≫ / *Edisto Revisited*

By Padgett Powell

Edisto (1984)
A Woman Named Drown (1987)
Typical (1991)
Edisto Revisited (1996)

EDISTO

REVISITED

／ *a novel*

PADGETT

POWELL

Henry Holt and Company

New York

The author gratefully acknowledges
Ledig House.

Henry Holt and Company, Inc.
Publishers since 1866
115 West 18th Street
New York, New York 10011

Henry Holt® is a registered
trademark of Henry Holt and Company, Inc.

Published in Canada by Fitzhenry & Whiteside Ltd.,
195 Allstate Parkway, Markham, Ontario L3R 4T8.

Library of Congress Cataloging-in-Publication Data
Powell, Padgett.
Edisto revisited / Padgett Powell.—1st ed.
p.   cm.
I. Title.
PS3566.O8328E34   1996   95-34071
813'.54—dc20   CIP

ISBN 0-8050-4237-7

Henry Holt books are available for
special promotions and premiums.
For details contact:
Director, Special Markets.

First Edition—1996

Designed by Cynthia Krupat

An Editor's Press Book: Pat Strachan

Printed in the United States of America
All first editions are printed on acid-free paper. ∞

10   9   8   7   6   5   4   3   2   1

For Ben Sonnenberg

❧ / *Edisto Revisited*

1 / I, SIMONS MANIGAULT, did not go to Harvard, following my mother's Quentin Compson, nor to Sewanee, following my father's footsteps and hopes. The titans of parenting came to a sorry compromise: I matriculated at Clemson, took a degree in architecture, which I could foresee never practicing but which was agreeable in the extreme against the prospect of reading for critical purposes the literature my mother bade me consume as a child. When you have read of Hester Prynne and her A as a bedtime story, more or less, you are not prepared to be waked up—and it is fancied a heady awakening—with it in a classroom. No, you are not.

My mother waked me to sleep, and I take my sleeping slow, as the poet with plenty of lying topspin did not put it, and I am inclined to a life of perennial nod.

I had some promise, it is said. It is not specified who promised what, of what the promise was made, where it inclined, on whom it bade well. Its bearing, its speed, its content I deem never adequately specified before I broke it.

I have a prurient mind, inclined once to what is called promiscuity, incline to what is called alcoholism, am insensitive to others' feelings, lack methods of self-preservation despite marked selfishness, am analytically slow, if not stupid, am badly undereducated, show evidence of moral and physical cowardice, and have a perennial spare tire about my soft gut. Beyond this there is not much wrong with me. I have all my hair and all my teeth.

The house I grew up in and lived to make much of as a child, with its surround of noises from the sea and its books—sand peppering the walls as I read my mother's bidding—is now, when I visit, a hot, dull, small place. My mother, for whom and for whose drinking I once had poetic locutions, is today a tired, ragged, happy drinker.

My old man goes every year for his prostate exam, to a doctor who is, of course, a childhood friend and Yacht Club colleague, and with whom he will have a drink not two hours after the fellow's latexed finger has been having a look. My father, it would seem, is notorious in the small ways that the prostate-vigilant can be: he will not wait for the doctor, who must remove his glove first, to procure him a tissue, but waddles hobbled to the stainless-steel box and grabs a handful of the coarse brown folded sheets and swabs out the scene and is buttoning up before the doctor's glove is off. My hallowed, vaunted heritage. I know the scene because the Yacht Club hears it once a year, instant replay— my old man wobbles for a napkin in the telling—and a story told once at the Yacht Club is told a thousand times in a thousand lesser places. On the issue of Jews, who are excluded from the Yacht Club, or the issue, specifically, of my having dated one, my father is a liberal: "All cats are black at night."

There you have it. A fellow as lugubriously sensitive as I was once alleged, and who may admittedly have served notice to that effect himself, would have killed himself. I suppose only familiarity with suicide poets—that I can thank my mother for—and in particular with young suicide poets, bred enough contempt that I declared the route invalid. I detoured into meanness. And into, I suppose it is fair to say, practicality. There is not going to be anything particularly horrifying about your old man talking about K-Y jelly and Jews and real estate in one breath, or your mother languishing of a broken literary heart, or your having your average career in venereal diseases and land-grant architectural programs. I avoid football games and do not make a point of fraternizing with members of other races. Other than that, I am properly collegiate in America. It is true that the proper do not know whom they have on their hands, but that is true, when you get down to it, of everyone. Or nearly everyone. Is it not?

•

Upon completion of my studies in drawing buildings, I put everything on the lawn of the dormitory and meant to set it on fire. Before I could effect this auto-da-fé, which was intended solely to reduce packing labors and those attendant labors at the other end, which are not simply unpacking labors but tasks of decision bearing on being itself—where to put this? Where that? Do I need these books *regularly*? There's only *five* plates. What sixth guest may I never invite?—a fellow came up and said he'd like to buy my drafting table (for a case of beer [$6.58], he did [table $298]); another got my hydraulic drawing stool ($6.58 for $342). A crowd gathered and drank the two cases of beer and absorbed everything I owned and sent me off hail and well met with my toothbrush in my oxford-cloth pocket, whistling those Henry Miller blues.

I was not the happiest man alive, but I was not far from it.

I broke into my girlfriend's apartment and worked all afternoon on Julia Child recipes, with more vigor jumping around to local radio rock-and-roll than even Julia on television, but drinking wine and cutting myself all the same, perfecting thereby my more sanguine *meunière*. I served Sheila seven subtle foods of the French cuisine and took my leave of her. I said something embarrassing to her. If you sing "Love Me Two Times" and "Light My Fire" all afternoon drinking all the Gallo with*out* Jim Morrison's erection and scrutinizing when the chicken breast is *springy* and when it is not, you may deliver yourself of an embarrassing *mot injuste*. I said to poor Sheila, "Had I gone to another school, I might have met . . . your wilder, worse sister." I meant by this that had I gone to Boston I'd have met a liturgical militant who scared me with things I don't know about, but I had, as a Clemson Tiger, met nice white-Jewish Sheila instead, who never did anything to me bad and whom I therefore was finally made too nervous by to hang around letting her take it—take all my inarticulate foggy incomprehension not directed at her or at anyone but simply swinging 360 degrees from a lofty tower in the unsympathetic goy fog. You see why I said only what I said to Sheila. She slid the door chain off gravely for me, and suddenly I had my toothbrush in the hall and I felt a little bad and a little real good.

I emerged onto a perfectly still, wet, wee-hour lawn, unlike Ted Bundy, not needing to run.

•

How I wish that I were a historian of The South. What not give for the opportunity to sit before documentary cameras in my cozy, musty Memphis study and relate lugubrious apocrypha about Rebel valor, with modest little tears in my wide delta face. There were twenty or so Union soldiers who had captured this one Southern boy, and they said, Why are you fighting us? He was not the sort, they could surmise, to be concerned with money or slavery. Because y'all are *down heah*, he says to them. *Which I think is a pretty good reason.* "Custer, a cap'n at the tiyeum," rode out into the Pickaninny River and "sat his horse and tunned and said, '*This* is how deep it is, Gen'el.' " What not give?

But I am not a historian of The South. I am arguably his worst enemy. The weepy little sons of bitches. My father is better company than a person who *believes* in The South. I should say he believes in where he is, it happens to be The South. He does not apotheosize The Lost World, confident of discovering yet in it the last baby Confederate dinosaur alive. Or tell you about it—how the baby Confederate dinosaur they spotted could not be captured—with that tear in his eye. I am not a historian-archaeologist of The South, I am an architect of no distinction who has recently tried to burn his T square and not managed that.

I bode to build no buildings. There are architects whose expertise lies in tearing them down.

The Wawer, the Wawer. They are right in longing for the Wawer, but they make a mistake in wanting the historical one: what we need is a new one, right here on this hallowed ground. Napalm on malls, uncontrollable Pampers looting. Can you imagine Ho Chi Minh offering to bomb *us* back into the Stone Age? His generals around the table slowly begin to chuckle. They may well have sufficient ordnance in the room.

After I got my useless degree and gave pointless pain to a good girl, I decided it was time to go home.

2 / I EXPECTED Going Home to See Mother to be a maudlin, necessary affair. There would be no non-obligatory moves. It would be the kind of ordeal wherein everything you do or say for days feels scripted in advance, and somehow everyone else seems unaware there is a script and yet appears agreeable to the proceedings entire. You gradually get the sense you are not altogether sane in entertaining this "script" delusion, that everything is, as every rational index suggests, perfectly fine, and that you'd best just *calm down*. In my anticipation of all this—the Homecoming Ritual—I thought of jumping script by *not* going, but even that seemed to be on a programmed template.

What started me thinking of inescapable behavior was the local military news: they were "discovering" lesbians at Parris Island again and giving them a God-and-country hard time. They had two of them apparently staked out in the center of the base and everyone was kicking sand at them and throwing spitballs at them and they were not going to get to be soldiers anymore. It just gave me pause: the whole objection to women being in the service in the first place was—was it not?—that the defense of the nation would degrade overnight into a panty raid. It would seem that the military would have *sought out* women not interested in men; would, at any rate, once it had them, prize them above the dangerous, seductive others. And on a lower kind of logic: I've been in enough lesbian bars to know you want a platoon of *them* fighting for you, not a division of debutantes chasing the boys on the other side. So. My conclusion? Join the Marines. What else?

These things never work. You cannot walk into the service. Weeks, months could be required. The form-filling-out itself would be sufficiently dull and long for you to ask what was so wrong, finally, with going home and drinking with your mother all night for a few weeks, or months, or even years? What was so wrong with that? I heard an Elvis champion at school, in the presence of a discussion of Mr. Presley's alleged taste for prepubescent girls, challenge the group: "Just what's wrong *with that*?"

So I did not stop at the recruiting station, which was in a two-hundred-acre mall and would have taken two hours to locate, and I went ahead with the script, and pulled in at the Baby Grand knowing, knowing, knowing You Can't Go to the Baby Grand Again, but going anyway. You must . . . you must try.

The reason you can't go home again is, of course, not that everything has changed but that almost nothing has changed. So Jake would not be absent, or dead; he would be at the bar, leg up and smoking, and he was. He would not *not* know you, or go into an I-declare and summon someone (a woman) who could second with a Lawd-have-mercy—no. He does not even bother to say, "Sim."

He comes up to me and I say, "A beer, Jake."

He stands there.

"Any kind."

He gets it. It is a Magnum malt liquor. I look at it.

"You say any kind." Jake smiles. It is nice to know he recognizes me. He smokes some more, back at his station. He times me and gets another one, looking at me to see if I am receiving. I am. He serves me the second one. "You back?" he says.

"I hope not," I say.

"I heard that."

"How's the house?"

"Y'all still have that?"

"I think we do."

"I don't know."

"What?"

"How it is."

"Oh."

I come to. My mother is not *in* the house. She is in Hilton Head. I have forgotten where my mother lives. The house I am going to see her in, going *home* to, is empty. I *can* go home again. It isn't home! What a pleasant surprise.

"Jake, how's your mother?"

"Died."

"Your . . . girl? I forgot her name."

"Gond."

"Got a new one?"

"Always got a new one."

He laughs a little here, a squarely cynical little chuckle.

3 / SO WHEN I GET THERE my mother will
not appear coyly doe-eyed at the screen door and say, Oh,
Son, come in—a drink? I will not accept one and lay myself
out on a wicker sofa opposite her, on one like mine, where
she does not *recline* as I, young man of the world, do, but
sits on her legs, folded up to the side of her like a girl. She
is half-lit by the conical play of lamplight from the end table
on which sits her drink, her cigarettes, her ashtray, and her
Charles Lamb or Richard Crashaw or Andrew Marvell, always a small, neat book with a good cloth or leather binding
and set at a deliberate, pleasing angle to the drink and the
cigarettes and the lamp. It is possible that we will not talk,
or that we will talk of something altogether odd. This last
is the preferred course, in lieu of nothing at all.

"The thing that worries *me*," she can say, if we go the
odd route, "is not *evil*—you sufficiently explained that to
me fifteen years ago—what worries me is *opportunity*."

"Yes, ma'am."

I know exactly what she means. It worries me, too. It
worries everyone except those with none of it, arguably the

happiest people alive. This is why baseball is the national sport, despite its being slower, duller, longer, and deader than its rivals. In baseball, opportunity is quantized and specified and the players *seize it* or not and win or lose accordingly. If you have an opportunity to *hit*, you hit; to *catch*, you catch. Very relaxing spectacle, in the hands of professional opportunity seizers.

I look at my mother. She is not a professional opportunity seizer. She's on Thompson Time, for one thing. That she has seized. I am not a professional opportunity seizer, either. I am an amateur opportunity seizer; that case could be made, but only because giant quantities of opportunity have fallen on me and I have been unable to dodge the fallout entirely. Thus I am an architect today, for example, and I can tell it is Coleridge on her end table, and I know what Samuel has to say about the universe containing more things invisible than visible (and he's right, of course, but how could he have known that *then*?).

"I sufficiently explained evil to you when I was . . . how old?"

"You did."

"Pray tell." Oh. Already my drink is good to me, too. Thompson Time is good time. I'm back to the sideboard as she delivers the explanation.

". . . and you said, 'Evil? That's an easy one, Mom. Without evil, dog wouldn't chase the cat, cat wouldn't climb a tree. Wouldn't be . . . *anything*.'"

"What prompted this thesis?"

"I told you evil was what I could not understand in this world."

"Why did you tell me that?"

"At the time, I *didn't* understand it."

I have my new drink, and we toast each other silently from our positions, and we would be lovers were the biology not considerably in the way.

•

But none of this will happen, because my mother will not be in the house when I get to it. I will unlock it and go in, walking on sand and bug carcass and the poppy seed of roach leavings. Announce myself to the Hook Man, or his adult equivalent. A man was discovered in this house by my father's sister, Sasa, several years ago. He had broken in, drunk all the liquor, passed out on one of the sofas, and was lying there when my aunt found him "with a peter *this big*," as she phrased it, putting her thumb on the second joint of her little finger and holding it in the air. The unfortunate's name was Wishmeyer. Today, entering the house, I call, "Time to head out, Mr. Wishmeyer. Get dressed." He has not come back. The house is empty, still, and stale. The linoleum cracks underfoot like .22s, as if it's frozen. The sand is nearly in *drifts*. How does this happen?

Except for the time it takes to open the house, admitting wind and the deafening relaxing noise of the surf, I act more or less as if my mother is present. I get that Old Thompson and sit down on my sofa and look at her spot on hers, turn on her lamp. Ashtray, no drink, no cigarette, no book. I sit back down. I miss her—oddly, I think at first, but then I see that I miss her only as if she were a lover. How nice to come to a house like this with a woman in it you could both talk to and have. I don't want just the one, either one, without the other. I am, as I say, an amateur at seizing opportunity.

I sat and regarded my position in the world, what was expected of me and what I expected. Was I going to be someone who cashed and wrote checks, on time and late, large or small, with those other check writers around him, in time and space until he died, or was I going to figure something out? Was I going to design buildings in Atlanta that either were on an address called Peachtree or had the word Peachtree on them, and be moderately well known in the *Southern Living* Who's Who, or was I going to snap my fingers and wake at 3 A.M. one night and agree on an obscure bit of rhetoric with Aristotle? I was going to have another Thompson clock winder before any of it.

At the sideboard I was enfiladed by an epiphany. The liquor in the cut glass looked like pine resin and it didn't smell much different. I looked in its amber facets. Liquor was a thing that dissolved you agreeably into place, into accepting, if not finally loving, the place you found yourself. It amounted to a magic potion that rendered any local hell into a species of heaven. That I knew about. That anybody who knew anything about liquor knew about. What was harder to see—possible only in rare lucid moments when looking at a decanter of whiskey become a slurry of pine resin—was that the passion for place itself was deluded; the idea that some configuration of geography, property, and the attendant means that secured it for you was going to satisfy you was lunatic. Geography is not going to satisfy. I thought of the lugubrious Wawer historians who thought that if only Mr. Sherman had not burned the hallowed salvation that was place. . . . The truth was, Sherman had nearly single-handedly liberated a clan of self-elected, inbred, unimaginative *white* slaves (slaves, to the second power, of place) from their central, crucifying delusion. And today a large Greek Revival portico with a sky-blue ceiling and forty outbuildings and landlocked seagoing fish in your hundred-year-old rice compounds and a cherry dining table thirty feet long and Merrill Lynch standing firmly behind it all is *still* not going to satisfy. As hard as that is to believe. And that is hard to believe. But looking into a liquor decanter, with liquor that looks like resin, and beautiful angles and refractions of my hand and of the room, its big empty breeziness a kaleidoscope of billowing drapes and knick-knacks, I believed it. I was once a student of literature. A character of whom I was fond makes a joke about this very epiphany. "You do not need to be justified," he says—he means it biblically—"if you have a *good car*." Drunk in my own beach house, I see that a good car, a good building, a good career, a good woman, a good . . . *anything*, will not justify me.

I wonder, before going to bed, if a revelation like this could lead to anorexia nervosa. Truth is, I have been a little overweight, right around the middle. On the other hand, one more drink and it would be time for breakfast—ravenous for eggs and bacon in the salt air, and seething resentment for General Sherman despite myself, and just about strung out enough to call someone up and weep on the phone about the Wawer. It's *all* attractive, on Thompson Time.

4 / THE NEXT MORNING I went down to
the shack. When you decide that place is fallacy, not part
of the solution to the vague, friendly unrest that we all have,
all who don't have specific, unfriendly unrest—and why
more of us do not have specific, unfriendly unrest I'd like
to know (did Elvis feel vague angst? No. The King did not.
He felt he needed many pills—what's wrong with that?—
and he felt he should have a bowel movement sometime
soon, to stay on his once-a-month schedule, which Nicho-
poulos Hippocrates had deemed adequate for a country boy
of durable stock)—what you do when possessed of the notion that place is not the answer is get meaner place, so I
went down to the shack.

It *was* mean. The tar paper had given up outside, dry,
gray rips of it showing rusty-nailed diagonal wood underneath, and inside, the newspaper was still on the walls but
it was very yellow, nearly tobacco-colored, and I found it
hard to believe I had once been able to read the stories. The
copy I had read easily as a child was not to be read now. I
didn't know if the yellowing had been accelerated by the

cabin's vacancy or what, or if, like the Sistine Chapel, it just needed a good wipe down. The shack smelled like a rat, a big, dry, clean, country rat, but still a rat. I closed it back up. In front of it was a chair and I took a seat. The surf was brilliant and rough and very pleasing. The sun was . . . round. I wanted something but did not know what. Why do we want what we do not know we want? Where did we pick this trick up? Is it the evolutionary mark of humanness? Imagine a dog, even a monkey, wanting something he just can't put his finger on. A broad-backed, ebony-faced lowland gorilla saying, "It's on the tip of my tongue . . ."

I want to know what is going on. That is what I want. Then I'd reason what to want. What is going on. What the big picture is here. It seems to me trivial whether you won or lost the Wawer, or like the Audi over the BMW, or are a lesbian staked out with wet-leather thongs by U.S. government Indians instead of a bride picking out her silver, if you don't have the big picture. I do not have the big picture.

What I have to do, I suppose, is not want the big picture. That would free me to elect the BMW, the Chantilly, the tomato futures, the European *Wanderjahr* (it's my time, I'm afraid), the partnership with the post-and-beam revival boys in Litchfield or the I-beam-and-skin boys in Atlanta; to contribute to the forest fund, elephant fund, whale fund, turtle fund, United Negro College Fund, UNICEF, Save the Children, Band-Aid, Pro-Life, Pro-Choice, choice, choice, choice.

The sand at the feet of the chair is damp, clean, squeaky in its shearing with my feet. It is like sugar, but tastes more, I know, of salt. A few million cubic tons of the world's finest rock salt. I'm on it. Squeaking my feet in it. This is the picture I have, the only picture I have. No one should have to suffer life with a head this small. There's a shark a hundred yards from me in four feet of water who could eat me alive, who knows more than I do. He certainly knows his big picture. Mr. Shark is a sharp and fortunate fellow.

I think of something yellow, yellow and tasty: it is time— the little picture comes in clear—for those eggs.

A phrase of my old man's: "Manage the screw-up quotient. That's what life is. Deft management of the screw-up quotient." But that son of a bitch knows what goes in the denominator and what goes in the numerator, and I do not. He knows what's going on, in other words. I dislike him. He's okay, you understand. But . . . no. There's another way. For now, soft scrambled eggs, heavy pepper, neat whiskey.

•

Before I get to discover there are no eggs or anything else solid in the house, the phone rings. I am accustomed to the answering machines of friends at school, the screens. We don't have a screening machine down here at the beach. I pick it up.

"I thought you'd be there," my mother says.

"I am."

"I can tell."

What? She's a drinker, not a drunk.

"*Your father*," she intones, "wants to go up for your commencement."

"Tell him I have commenced."

"He won't have it."

"Sure he will. Tell him to come down here and plan my future. That's what he really wants to do. Tell him I have commenced the planning."

She laughs—much more herself.

"I plan to scramble some eggs. I plan to have you all restock the liquor larder. I plan to wear a pink dress when he gets here. I plan hallucinations. Seriously, there's no real booze here. Why don't you come down?"

"Athenia had a stroke."

"What?"

"Athenia had a major stroke. They say she'll never move her left side again. I don't know how they know that."

"I thought you didn't know where she was."

"I didn't. They surface."

"Seems they do."

The hangover I did not have when squeaking clean ocean sand I suddenly have listening to details of the incarceration of the invalid poor. The state has named a holding facility for the invalid poor Turtle Creek. I will be going, imprudently, but as certainly as I stand with a phone in one hand trying to massage both temples with the other, to this Turtle Creek. As carefree as a white rabbit, I will be going to Turtle Creek to see some hopelessness, some urine where you wouldn't think it fair.

"Mom"—she's talking about something—"Mother, that fellow who served paper down here? Involved with Theenie leaving, it seemed? Her daughter, or something—"

She says something that again makes me wonder if Thompson Time is all the time: "Blue suede shoes. Don't judge me."

"What?"

"I wouldn't go."

"Go where?"

"To see Athenia."

"I know you wouldn't. But you're telling me so I can go. I am the naïf. That's my job in this outfit, is it not?"

"What are you talking about?"

"I was wondering what happened to that guy—"

"I don't know what happened to that guy."

She's very deliberate, careful, betraying herself in the repetition. She's sensitive about this old lover. I was right all along. She might as well be a schoolgirl trying to conceal a crush. I could ask her point-blank about others and get a straight answer, I think. I think to try her.

"Hey!"

"What!"

"Where is Jules Windham these days?"

"Selling funerals for Bilo Windham, as always."

Yes.

"Do you want to hear about Turtle Creek if I go?"

"No."

"Don't let anyone know I'm here. Tell him I'm in Atlanta looking for a job. I will be there looking for a job until further notice."

"Where will you be?"

"Right here. Looking for a job."

"Good."

The Doctor hangs up. She likes the idea of that son of hers holed up in an empty house. I don't mind it myself. There are lots of jobs here—small ones that contribute directly to human comfort, such as removing the snowdrifts of sand and locating fresh eggs and fresh liquor, and large, cerebral ones that contribute directly to discomfort. I shall do a bunch of the small and a few of the large. Blue suede shoes, indeed. Do not step, I inform the Atlantic Ocean, on my blue suede shoes.

5 / IT DOES NOT MATTER that I have not seen Theenie in some fifteen years, but I think it will matter when I wade into the halls of misery at Turtle Creek. Important, important to spot her in her wheelchair from twenty yards and smoothly, directly, confidently approach her, with a smug I-knew-you'd-be-parked-right-here look and an athletic grade into squatting during the final approach so that you land at her level, a hand on her arm to prevent more awkward intimacies or awkward lack of other intimacies. This business—intimacy warding off—you see the importance of when you walk in and a woman in a wet nightgown, backlit so you see her skeleton through it, declares, "Help me! What took you so long!" and approaches with her arms outstretched and with the determination of a living-dead zombie, and you look to the attendant escorting you to dissuade the woman, and the attendant politely steps back to let the woman have at you. You politely ease behind the attendant, who says, "What the matter with you?"

"I don't know that woman."

"They *change* in here, child."

"I'm looking for a *black* woman. They change that much?"

The attendant chuckles and abruptly leaves, and you, a step later, follow, the begging woman not two feet away with her outstretched arms. Every patient—you've already been told they are not to be called inmates—who can recognize anything recognizes you as someone dear to her, all the way down the halls and through the big rec rooms.

I mistook two or three patients to be Theenie because I did not want to disappoint her by not recognizing her. Picturing her heavier or lighter, her hair perhaps thinner, bluer, her teeth perhaps gone—it was easy to see her in three or four other failing black women in wheelchairs. On the basis of one visit I will hazard a racial generalization: Incapacitated white women are indignant, certain of rescue, depressed, and angry; the black women beside them are at peace, not anticipating rescue, and not angry. They are not saying, in their postures and grasping and yelling, If we'd known it would come to this. . . . They are saying, *We* knew it would come to this. Somebody help them white bitches. Make 'em *shut up*.

So there I am.

"Which?" the attendant is saying.

"None which in here," I say. I'm tired of this woman laughing at me, and I'm going to use a little language to fend her off.

"What her name again?"

"Athenia Small."

"Small. Small."

"Small."

"She new?"

"I don't know."

"Come on."

I seem to have gained a measure of respect, or credibility, I can't tell. There are things going on here I can't even apprehend, let alone comprehend, I'm sure—I'm likely to start crying, for one thing. There is something profoundly wrong with acres of women weeping and fouling themselves and recognizing salvation in strangers. I get the feeling there is something unusual in visiting itself, but beyond that that there are not too many white boys coming to see a black woman, unless it's some kind of odious, sentimental thing just like my visit is. This boy she raised come in once, they will say. "They" are the black women at the desk. Behind them, hidden, somewhere, are the white men in charge. I am one of them, in the final scheme of things. I know this, but in an atmosphere of confusion—a woman on the floor here, one weeping into drapes here, one addressing invisible kitties here, and all through all of it the urine smell—in this atmosphere I don't feel like acknowledging any racial deferences or subtleties. I am in a place where survival is the issue, and everyone but me and my bossy, chuckling escort has missed the boat, and I am worried not about the delicate social minuet between me and her but about me getting out intact.

We turn into a room.

"That her?"

It is. Unmistakably; though depredations there have been. I cross to Theenie and deliberately do not acknowledge my escort. Theenie recognizes me instantly and tries to say, "Lord! Who is that? I raised you but I don't know who you is! You ain't been to see your Theenie in . . . a criminal time. Like you a secret. What is you, a milintary secret? Come on in. You want a Coke?" It does not come out that way. Her right arm, which resembles a deer's leg drawn up by a slow fire, and the left side of her face, drawn down toward her shoulder by a permanent spasm of muscle, move rhythmically, and a sound comes out of her, but it is a sound I have heard only once before, from a dog hit by a car. Hurt badly but not killed, it sat on its useless hind legs and waved its head and moaned.

6 / SHE'S TUCKED IN, in a neat hospital bed, but a smell hits me and I detect damp edges of the sheets and have small outrage—what is wrong with catheters? I turn to the escort to make some demands and she is, of course, gone. This would be difficult enough, Theenie and I alone doing whatever we are to do, but there's more: a woman I just now notice, sitting in the corner, stands up and approaches me very formally. She is well dressed and so self-possessed that it occurs to me she may be the mysterious administration herself. "I'm Athenia's sister," she says, and shakes my hand.

"I didn't know she had a sister," I say.

I glance at Athenia, who is more agitated now than when I walked in. Her eyes are reeling from side to side and she is trying to talk.

"May I see you outside?" the woman asks.

"Certainly."

I give Theenie a gesture of conspiratorial assurance that I am just humoring this woman, anticipating correctly, somehow, that what she—Athenia—is trying to say is, the woman is *not* her sister.

Out in the hall, the woman makes a presentation that convinces me she *is* a sister. It goes something like this:

"I assume you are one of the families she has worked for. Am I right? Well. This is distressing—"

"I didn't know Athenia had family."

"That does not surprise me. She removed herself from us many years ago. She had everything. It has been a mystery and a painful thing for us. She threw away . . . she did not have to do with her life what she did. And now—"

"She did not have to work . . . as a maid?"

"No. My father had a lot of money, in—"

"But you'd think she'd have *mentioned*—"

"She is inscrutable. Here."

She hands me a business card, her husband's, a dentist in Florida. I look at the woman. The resemblance is there. I recall the one piece of family about Athenia there was: a portrait of her mother wearing a headdress of some kind that suggested very vaguely to me as a child, and I can be no more specific now, "the islands."

I am back in the room, the woman having granted us a private session. Athenia cannot move her mouth or talk in any way, but she manages to say, with her eyes and some breath, clamping my hand with her good one, "Not my sister."

"I know."

She shakes her eyes back and forth—her No, I am learning.

I go into diagnostic check mode. Her Bible is by the bed.

"Can you read?" I ask.

Eyes say No.

"Even if it were held up for you?"

No.

"I take it you can understand everything said to you?"

Eyes don't move: Yes.

"Well."

Yes. Well. What now? I am a tit on a boar hog, is what now. Of what value am I? I, whose family employed this woman for twenty years, standing here like a mourner at a funeral, who has not to this point had the wit to see that the woman claiming to be a wealthy sister is the salvation if there is one . . . and the woman claiming to be the sister is gone. She has stepped out for a snack or she has stepped out for a plane to Florida, her mission, whatever it was, abrupted and altered by me. And not inappropriately, I think: white people have been in that woman's way all her life, in a way directly opposite to the way her sister, Athenia, had them in *her* way. I am in the middle of a large political and racial family spat, with some bizarre contours to it, if Theenie has *elected* servitude as the woman suggests. If she has thrown things away: and that is a terrible thought, when the woman making the accusation has the demeanor of a bank president and the throwing-away accused had the demeanor of a bandannaed Jemima, *before* her veins blew out. I am made a little nervous by these speculations. Worrying about catheters and euthanasia was easy compared to this. I want to run, withal, before any more can happen, and basically, I do.

If you have emptied yourself of sympathy, you get blunt. I say to Theenie: "Athenia, this looks pretty bad."

Eyes still.

"But you told me the solution years ago."

Eyes still.

"You don't have to do anything in life except die and live till you die."

Eyes still, then back and forth.

I wonder if it is not, somehow, salubrious news. All she has to do is rot in sores and piss until she dies, and I have told her so.

·

On the curb, outside, I discover I am not empty of sympathy. It is that you must distrust sympathy, and cruelty is more suitable. Sympathy is the only emotion you have in a Turtle Creek, and it will overwhelm you if you let it, and you would be, though perhaps medically more fit, no more mentally adept at survival than the patients, among whose wheelchairs you would go down in a weeping heap. On the curb I look at the gutter which my feet hang over as if I am surfing. I could start crying if I allowed myself to, and not stop. If you were to start, you would not stop.

·

If you start things in life, the likelihood is you will not stop. That is the sum and the summit of what I know today, teetering before careerhood, having taken up hermiting in a beach house, erstwhile the house I grew up in. I certainly see nothing to obstruct this most agreeable hermitage. I can see from this salty vantage, lounging around on grit and noting repairs necessary to the house but not about to effect them, that you must be careful in life not to begin things you do not wish to do for a long time. The gravity of habit looks perdurable and instantaneous. I hesitate—for one low-minded and trivial example—to replace the hinge on the shutter by the sideboard. It is one of, looks to be, ninety-one more hinges, none in top condition.

Here's another trivial example: With the purchase of one pair of Kelly-green poplin slacks and with one phone call to my father telling him I'd like to belong to Hilton Head Pines Country Club, he'd secure me membership, a bag of pro-grade clubs you'd need a caddie or a cart to carry for you, and I would golf at HHPCC and other clubs of similar status from here through Georgia and North Carolina for the rest of my life. *Member-guest tournament* would be a permanent, recurring phenomenon in my days on Earth.

7 / MY MOTHER IS at the house when I get back from my little lesson in first and last things at Turtle Creek. This is what she meant by "good," when I told her I'd be holing up: she can, too. In the backseat of her car is a case of liquor and what looks like a Smithfield ham. She is a good one for provisions, laying them in and savoring the larder. She'd be good on a ship.

I take up a load—there are sacked groceries, too—and hear from the kitchen the shower going. My mother will emerge with a towel on her head, Nefertiti fashion, and a good terry-cloth robe, and make herself a tall gin-and-tonic and look like a movie star for an hour. Being around her is like being on safari; there is an elusive something we are after, in difficult conditions, and we will look good in the getting there. She can manage to snuggle into the world where ordinary people would languish. She will look like a lion hunter with a small glister of country-ham fat on her lip and the fine spray of fresh carbonated tonic dancing in the air before her bright eyes. And she will taste the salty meat and the tart tonic and gin and lime and settle into the crisp wicker with a contentment that is agreeably restless: *What now?* she says, smiling.

I don't know, but something, you say, agreeably slapping your thigh, both of you shaking your heads together at the mystery of nothingness about you and your lives. My mother is a very accomplished safarigoer. We have never determined the game we are after, is the only small problem. It doesn't bother her, and she instructs me not to let it bother me.

Before she comes out, before I have the limes sliced—I am putting up corned beef and saltines and sardines and maraschino cherries and Ovaltine and cheese and Wheat Thins: it's like Christmas going through the groceries, no Turtle Creek *here*—a sound comes from my bedroom.

The kind of disappointment this could suggest is large. I dread that it is a beau, as she likes to call them. The situation is complex and long and tedious; suffice it to say, here, that it could be a beau, that I do not want it to be, I do not want to share any of this good load of groceries with a boyfriend of my mother. That's not all there is to it, but that's enough.

I poke my head in the room, and on the bed, reclined with feet crossed, arms behind head, is a woman, about a thirty-year-old-looking woman that I feel I should recognize. It's a rather smart-looking woman, trim, tasteful, sturdy. I find it difficult to leave, standing against the doorjamb with a knife and a lime.

"Hi," she says, eyes open.

"Hi."

"Remember me?"

"Yes."

"There *wasn't* really a snake. I wanted you to save me."

"Did I save you?"

"No."

My mother is emerged. "You've found your cousin," she says from across the way.

"Yes, I have."

"She turned out well, didn't she?"

My cousin, on the bed yet, looks directly at me with, I swear, a caricature of sultriness in her expression.

"She did," I call to my mother over my shoulder.

"You did," I say to this woman they are calling my cousin.

"I know I did," she says, still in the charade of allure, I think.

But I cannot be sure it is charade. I may well be looking at a cousin of mine in an inviting pose on my own bed who does think she turned out well. The fact is, she *has* turned out well, very very well, so well that at least two people in a house of three think the strange woman on my bed has turned out well, and the woman on the bed seems inclined to go along, if only in farce. A woman who turned out well on my bed! My mother for chaperone! Don't have to share the sardines with an oaf who paws my mother! What a day!

I go down to the car to get the ham. I shall carve the ham, and the ladies and I shall eat the ham. There's enough lust and food and liquor and good weather and sea breeze and iodine on that breeze and good-looking women on hand to think life a perfect piece of cake there for the eating. Life, suddenly, is an *I can't wait* proposition.

•

When she was twelve years old, my turned-out-well cousin—tonight sitting opposite me on the sofa with my mother and with her legs out in an elegant scissoring cross, not folded up under her as my mother's are—my turned-out-well cousin, whom I want badly and see is possible to be had, given judicious application of charm and feigned indifference, and given her just detectable suggested recent history of some not-working-out with a man, some kind of failed fling that she is working hard not to allow to be major, to reduce to misdemeanor, an annoyance, something laughable as she sits in the good ocean air with her entertaining low-country aunt, thinking, maybe, Aren't these two a pair, and Simons, how bitter and cute *he* turned out . . . ah, *the beach*, he's really rather . . . well, *grown-up*, to be just out of college. And I am wondering what Aunt he-had-a-peter-this-big Sasa's position would be if . . . I mean, we all know the historical low-country position on the matter of cousins *marrying*, but that *is* historical, not now, and marriage isn't what I am inclined to consider: I need a vacation, is what I need. My cousin, when she was twelve years old, admits to heavy false terror, terror struck in her by a snake she claimed to have seen that she claimed was at least seven feet long, frantically exiting the water—an upcountry lake—clutching her neck and screaming and coming to me hysterical with the news. Which news I apparently smartly dismissed as herpetologically impossible and went about my way, missing thereby the opportunity to console my then budding-breast cousin. Perhaps some private tenderness would have been in order, she says tonight, laughing. I have forgotten the incident entirely except for the image of her holding her neck, which gesture at the time I ascribed to choking on lake water before she spoke of the mythic snake.

But some fifteen years later the prospect of private tenderness in the way of consolation is not to be dismissed. There is again an hysteria obtaining in this woman, my cousin, quieter but also more real, and hysteria is a gold mine of opportunity in my limited experience—perhaps the sublimest atmosphere for negotiations on matters sexual between consenting adults. With at least one party hysterical, things go smoothly, smoothly.

Without saying a word, my mother is managing to contribute favorably and seriously to my cause. She sits there, twinkling of eye above her glass when she drinks, saying, *Of course* you claimed to have seen a seven-foot monster in order to attract my son, and—she keeps just twinkling, and the story itself does not merit it—*of course* you are telling us the story *tonight*. My mother is virtually winking at me, and then winking at my cousin: I understand, she says to her; you go right ahead.

What has arranged the presence of my cousin now does not get broached, which is what prompts me to suspect some kind of trouble that the league of women has agreed to keep to itself. Namely, in this case, from me, which is a boon to operations. I am free to be fresh. The shadow of palled relations with men has not been penumbrated unto me. I am in the sunshine. More correctly, I am in the sea breeze and the moonshine, and I am carving the ham. I take a good long look at my long-lost cousin Patricia, and I deduce that her good long legs have got that way riding horses. We have a Piedmont horse girl at large in the house, her genealogy preapproved, wanting to dash some small misery to pieces while down here. And I am the dashing man. To prove it, I fix them fresh drinks before they ask, and neglect my own, the better to watch women on firewater. If there is anything more interesting to watch than women on firewater, I do not know what it is.

•

There is talk of relatives I know not too well—too many of them to know them any better from listening to the run-down. A whole section of the family tree is pruned and primped and assessed as I politely sit there. Overall, I detect that the tree is fine: its leaves gently turning in the breeze of life. We have no scandal blight, no limb-wrenching storms of fate, no bad apples. I wonder what it is like when the Kennedys sit around for a disk check like this. You know they can always start at the good stuff and never move far from it. We are not the Kennedys, it would seem. We are the Manigaults. Well, two hundred years ago we had more rice than the Kennedys have votes. Buckra not on top today, is all. The Wawer. The Kennedys need them a Wawer, and I guess they've been having one all along.

There is a lull, and I am caught looking at Patricia. There is no profit in looking away. She looks steadily and directly and tellingly back, and she throws in some of that cartoonish voluptuousness and smiles a little in recognition of it, to tell me it is camp. I am most encouraged, delighted by her wit. The wit to say things, to render things easy, to preclude blunder. To be acting this way is, in my view, worthy of my affection as well as my lust. I begin to love this Patricia. This Patricia plays by some fair rules. This Patricia *plays*. This Patricia.

I busy myself in the kitchen, wrapping the ham, which tomorrow goes in the bathtub. We can't eat these nitrites for a whole ham.

"What firm in Atlanta do you have an in with?" my mother wants to know.

"Fitzsimmons, Trammell, and Blode," I tell her.

"And who in . . . is it Georgetown?"

"Litchfield. A guy who smokes pot and wins awards." It is true.

I hear her relate this—that I have, despite appearances, real direction in the world—to Patricia. I then hear talk of my father, in appropriately perfunctory tones and abbreviated rhythm. This will tell Patricia that I, too, struggle against the world of men. I take a look through the serving window at Patricia. Her head is back, as if she's not altogether listening. Someone has seen fit to deliver me a fine woman in my own house.

"Patricia's in your room," my mother announces. "You're in the front room."

"Fine. Ladies," I announce, "I shall take a constitutional on the beach. Leave the door unlocked." Patricia's expression is so perfectly neutral I fall in love, if not with her, with her face and what she can do with it. In my experience, loving a face is sufficient, but not necessary.

8 / I HOPED THAT she would make it easiest
of all and take a beach constitutional herself. I could have
just met her head-on and greengowned her, wind and surf
noise too much to bother with any subtle talk. I went down
to the shack and posted myself in the chair. The next ab-
surdly easy piece in the puzzle of seduction would be to bed
down with her in the shack, rat funk miraculously gone or
insignificant in the face of our giant strangers' passion. But
she did not come. It may well be that she came down and
looked around and, not seeing me, went back up; the shack
is out of sight up the beach. Poor logistics on my part. I
should have announced I was taking a constitutional *up* the
beach, 150 yards north to the chair beside the shack in
which, despite the rat smell, a couple of a mind to could
secure their new lust for each other on a simple poor pallet
and have theyselves a good time. But I did not. And sitting
in the chair watching the desolate turbulence and phos-
phorus and being blown nearly over backwards, I counsel
myself about putting mind in gear before mouth in motion.

Courage now will need be screwed into one scary ball, and I must dribble that ball into her (my) room, if I want to play.

•

I want to play. The absolute nadir of eventuality? She screams *rape*, and my mother condescendingly puts her on a bus in the morning and clucks about naïfs when she gets home. Somewhat less improbable, and more damaging to esteem, this Patricia simply is surprised and finally not interested, leaving me with an endless analysis of how I misread all that camp voluptuousness all night and might-should check in for some IQ work somewhere. At the top end, she says about what half the women at Turtle Creek said to me: What *took* you so long?

I make goodly noise going into the dark house, fiddle in my temporary room, a little wash up, turn down my temporary bed, turn off my temporary light, and go to my (her) room, my upcountry cousin's temporary bed. The door is closed. I open it, wide, and slowly enter, and slowly close it, not muffling the click. She does not move, but I do not hear the breathing of sleep: I am, we are, beyond the screaming point. The best way to get past the surprise point is to give her something to *be* surprised at; I don't speak, I sit, easily, on the bed. She puts a hand on my thigh.

"Hi," she says.

"Hi."

"Thought you might be gay."

"Apparently I'm not."

"Are you taking advantage of me, or me you?"

"You me."

"But you're *in* here."

"It's *my* room."

"Are you an alcoholic?"

"Not yet."

"Your mother's nice."

"She holds up, yes."

"The reason I'm here . . ."

"Yes?"

"Well, among others, I thought *I* was gay."

"But you're not?"

"Not yet." And she laughed, and in that release I kissed her. In a couple of minutes, for a couple of hours, we could have both been gay, I do not think we knew or cared. It was a storm. She was firm and she used her firmness. Femininity, or that softness that passes for it popularly, has no place in bed.

•

Somewhere about three in the morning I asked, "What's the plan here?"

"The plan?"

"How long you down for?"

"Don't know. All summer, I think."

That looked, at that moment, a delicious and correct period. All summer.

"Go to sleep, then."

"Okay."

"Night."

"Night."

A very tender and not self-conscious kiss. Gratuitous affection between adults is to my mind something you do not make fun of. The one thing you do not make fun of. I was, it is fair to say, wound up. The lust was tamped down for the moment, but tenderness and flutters were running high. She *tasted* good. She looked good. She made sense. I felt I had been agreeably run over, and I was agreeably getting twisted up underneath whatever vehicle it was; it was heavy and moving fast and had a two-range transmission like a rock truck. Trash was raining off the truck—"I thought I was gay"—and I did not care. Let it rain. Let there be trash. Intelligent, surviving animals make durable nests of trash. Trash is a precious commodity in our time. He who cannot look trash in the eye is lost. In a raiment of minor garbage walks the necessary hero today. Excuse me. It used to be a habit of mine, the boyish, untethered locution. Finding a woman in your bed can make a boy of you again, a cute, frisky boy.

•

When I woke up I was against the wall, looking over my cousin at the surf outside the window. Patricia Hod was looking straight up at the ceiling, unblinking, in a fixed eerie stare that would have given me the creeps if her eyes had not been themselves beautiful. They were the same blue as the ocean and the sky beyond them. She stared at the ceiling as if she knew about this marvelous optical com-position. But of course she did not, and I touched her. She gave my hand a little squeeze, still not looking from the ceiling or even blinking, and smiled. I was relieved and not: she was okay, the squeeze and smile said, but staring at the ceiling (for how long?) said not. I kissed her neck just below her jaw, which is what you do in situations like this.

A little awkward but delicate affection will secure a doubtful woman staring at the ceiling.

Her eyelashes stuck brightly and smartly up and out at angles from her eyeballs so that her eyes looked like miniature crowns. I thought of Orphan Annie. I watched her eyes gaze at the ceiling and held her hand and saw beyond, unfocused, the cool, rough, glassy morning surf thrash and roll and shine. Nothing could be finer than to be in Caroliner in the morning is about the way it felt.

9 / I RESOLVED in the morning to try not to be so *small*. I know where to get more detailed self-improvement lists—Mr. Franklin's comes to mind—but, for me, this is enough. I am supposed to be thinking about self-determination, about not wasting a life, about the large picture, and I am thinking about Patricia Hod's early ass in my late bed. My old lady is asleep and my new girlfriend is asleep. Weather fair. Tide regular. Boats on the horizon. Birds afloat and a-peckin'.

Patricia and I had a conversation somewhere in our parade of appetite about her taking me for gay. I asked her if she was serious. "Well," she said, "not really, I mean, I hoped . . . see, I've found this a lot—*a lot*—lately, that if a guy isn't, you know, Billy Carter, you can find him in the other camp. A lot. This has *something* to do with my entertaining—I thought I loved a woman."

"Because gays turn up?"

"Because Billy Carters kept turning up, more."

"I see." I thought maybe I did. "There's sexists on the one hand, like me, and gays on the other—"

"And in the middle, dweebs. You're not sexist."

"I thought if you openly pursued women for sex you were sexist."

"You are. But *you're* not."

"I don't see how not."

"Trust me."

Trust her I did: I kissed her, and we were done with this little minuet. Why I relate it now I'm not sure. Patricia Hod is a very accomplished kisser.

•

I sweep the house. I turn up furniture on other furniture and throw out the throw rugs and locate a good, new-looking broom. There is something eminently pleasing about coaxing sand over hardwood floors, a fine whispering pumicing, while the women sleep. The place will look, and feel, new when they get up. I am son, cousin, lover, innkeeper. Is this life's wasting or not wasting? The women will emerge in their safari khaki with their tired but expectant, hopeful safari faces on, tightening their belts. Camp coffee will be ready for them. Take pride in yourself, their bearings will instruct anyone who looks at them. We may not ever see a single lion, but we take pride in ourselves. Do not let your dogs get fat.

I oil the griddle—my mother had the wit to pick up a used commercial stove—and put bacon on it. Cholesterol to go with alcohol; all the bad things in English-speaking life end in *-ol*. Let's take this pistol and have us a little folderol. And eat this Demerol.

"Son?" It's an odd sound coming through the still house full of upended chairs. I go to her room.

"Ma'am?"

"Beer. Miller. Bottle."

"Tall order, Mother."

"It's a deathbed request. It *must* be in the bottle."

Were she less absurd, it would be an annoyance. Procuring a Miller in the bottle at eight in the morning is not an annoyance. It is a necessary detail in the correct safari that the women know more about than you do. I drive to Jake's.

Jake now has a door on the Grand that would look like a bank-vault door were it not made of wood. I knock, hoping not to have to go back to his house. Things have changed since I hiked to his house to dig fishing worms—women and dogs and racial climate and I have changed. It would be better to be a front-door customer now. A door within the door opens, a small deep trapezoidal passage like something on an old ice-cream truck. Jake's face is where you would see the Fudgsicles.

"Yeah?"

"Need beer."

"Closed."

"Jake. Miller in the bottle."

"She back."

"You know it."

"She a *pain* in the ass."

He's infected with it, too. Were she less a pain, were I just a drunk wanting something to drink, were there not in this picture a reclined woman commanding the bottled version of a white man's beer, one arm over her eyes and the other extended in space for the drink, Jake would say to hell with it. Were she *not* a pain in the ass, it would be no go. It is a go.

"Don't even carry this shit no more," he says, letting me in. The club is a ruin.

"What happened here?"

"Where?"

"This."

"What?"

"These people kill each other in here?"

"Nobody kill nobody."

My act needs a little pointing up, I detect. I know that, but the place did look . . . really *gone*.

While sacking the beer, Jake says, "Somebody fell down."

"I *thought* so," I say, with an intentionally self-righteous thrust which, I hope, will be comic.

Jake chuckles—he gets it. I am white boy playing white boy—not just white boy. It is a relief to be back in the groove. But I can see it will be a shallower groove than it was for me as a child. Get too cute now and I will be a clown like anyone else.

"She down for a while?"

"It looks like it. I don't know."

"You want three?" He means another six-pack, which he is ready to add to the two he's sacked.

"No. I'll come back. I don't even have money for those two. *Jake*."

"What?"

I can't contain myself. "I have a new girlfriend."

"Yeah?"

"*Brand*-new. *Last night*."

It is absurd for me to say this to him or to anyone else, but it comes out, and the absurdity helps in here, as usual, rather than hinders.

Jake smiles. "Last night?"

"Yes."

"Somebody you know?"

"Somebody I *don't* know."

"*Man*," he says. "Accidental sugar."

"Yes, sir."

"Accident the best."

"It must be."

"It is, son. Accident save your life. Even a young life like you, accident help."

"It does help, Jake."

"Happy for you."

I'm gone with the Miller in the bottle, feeling like some kind of traveling salesman with the punch line coming around the corner. The joke will be at my expense, but I do not care. I have suffered an accident of the gravest kind.

10 / COMING AROUND the corner of our road onto the hard road, in her infamous fashion, is my mother in her rock-blasting Cadillac, a thirty-year-old model that would be valuable were there any body whatsoever left on it.

We ease up window-to-window.

"I *have* the beer," I say.

"You took too long." She extends her arm. I hand her one bottle of beer. She laughs.

"That's all I'm giving you."

"Listen, I've got to go up. I was just bringing Patricia down here. She—we are sheltering her."

"From what?"

"Sasa is drinking badly and Winn called and asked if we would."

"Grown girl can't bear a toot?"

"Bit more to it. She was going to be home for the summer, and now is not. That's the short of it. Did your father buy you that car?"

"No."

"Good."

"He fixes it, though."

"Good. Perfect. You helpless scion. Your cousin is also helpless. It's a match made in helplessness."

"Is this official?"

"No. She's with me. If anyone calls, I'm with her. I'm just out."

"How long you out for?"

"Forever."

I swear to God my mother at this point attempts a high five between the windows of our cars. We don't quite pull it off, and laugh. I give her the six-pack she's broken. "Jake thinks fondly of you still."

"Jake. That's a good man, Jake."

"He speaks of accidental sugar."

"Damned poet in a jook."

"Yes."

"Well. Congratulations. On graduating. Now learn something."

With that she floors it out of our lane onto the hard road and catches rubber on the asphalt. I'm helpless, got helpless woman at the house, aim to learn something, ease on down the palmetto gauntlet to get with it.

Patricia Hod is on the back steps with a cup of coffee. Her legs look better even than I imagined they'd look. She does not appear altogether happy.

•

I sat next to her and proffered the beer. She declined.

"We're supposed to learn something. Dr. Manigault's instructions."

"God help us."

I touched her leg.

"Don't ever touch me in the morning."

"Couldn't help it. How'd you get those?"

"What?"

"Legs."

"These?" She looked at them, leaning over sideways, as if inspecting a pair of shoes she was considering. I decided to drop it. There were less dumb things to talk about, surely.

"Where'd you get that mouth?" she asked.

"All right." I didn't know if she meant how it looked, what I did with it, or what came out of it, but she'd made her point. We were coming together as Jesus flang us. We were as-is items on a yard-sale table. Affection was gratuitous. Captivity was assumed.

"Your mother's on a toot, I hear."

"My mother's an *ass*," she said with some force.

"She doesn't touch you in the morning."

"Brief miracle."

"Where were you?"

"When?"

"Before going home."

"London."

"And?"

"Some trouble."

"Ah." I said this as if I understood.

"I swam the English Channel, if you want to know where I got these legs."

"I read *Moby-Dick* when I was nine years old."

"Any rip currents out there?" She indicated the surf.

"Current out there suck you into Parris Island, put you in the lesbian brig."

"Funny. Excuse me."

She went in the house. When she emerged she was in a Speedo and cap-and-goggle headdress and she walked down the steps, looked at the wrecked Carrier compressor, raised her brows at me as if to say, Shouldn't that thing be in working order if we're to cohabit without a serious outbreak of cabin fever?, walked smoothly into the surf, swam north once the breakers left her alone, and was out of sight relatively quickly because I refused to turn my head to follow, acknowledge the elegance and horselike power with which she pulled all this off. I set to making club sandwiches and thinking about what I was going to do with myself, seriously, now that I apparently had a woman who knew what to do with herself. That changes things a bit.

11 / THE WOMAN WHO KNEW what to do with herself came in an hour later with a man-of-war sting on her calf, claiming she nearly drowned because there were so many washed ashore up the beach, she had to swim back.

"You get that," I said. "The purple and red, stringy tide."

"What makes you . . . so superior?" she said, very casually, and accenting the word—"superior"—in such a way that it didn't sound altogether like an accusation.

"I sound *superior?*"

"You don't try to. But you do."

"It's because, madame, I'm inferior."

"Too easy."

"Shall I modify behavior to suit my cousin on the lam from unspecified trouble abroad and at home?"

"There you go."

By this at first I thought she meant *There you go, being superior,* but she took a big bite of sandwich, looked up at the ceiling to contain an errant dollopette of mayonnaise at one corner of her mouth, and pushed it in with her little finger. She said no more, so that I decided "There you go" meant *That's the solution, do modify behavior, for me.*

"Okay," I said, fully intending any modification she felt in order, and knowing none would obtain. People do not change behavior, though they do, of course, popularly label a lot of their behavior changed, when some of it has been deemed in need of such a label. A person is as capable of a true change of behavior in equal degree to a planet's capacity to change its orbit.

"Patricia Hod," I say, "forgive me this, but I want your—" I couldn't say it.

"My bod?"

"Dante made me configure that trope."

"Understandable. There was a girl at school named Trott the boys just had to call Twat."

She leaned over the expert lay of smart club sandwiches and kissed me: mayonnaise, bacon, and salty girl. Or: tongue tomato tart and salty lip of girl. Or: tart tomato, salty lip, and woman.

12 / PATRICIA HOD and I did not go the distance, or anything like the distance, whatever the distance means these days. But we had what might be called a good preliminary, of about four rounds. Round one was even carnal scrapping (bliss); two was revelation on her part that the lesbian experimenting was related to bad weather with all her men; three was my supplying evidence that bad weather was in me; four was her confiding that one of her busted affairs had left her briefly catatonic with grief (*vide supra* staring at ceiling) until she came out of it and painted her appliances, and the sidewalk outside, orange, and drowned the cat before setting the apartment containing the orange toaster and popcorn popper and smoothie blender on fire. This last business engendered in me the opinion—I've heard boxing strategies called "opinions"—that the safest thing for me, dash honor, was not to answer the bell for any more rounds. I got nervous, and that was it. A lover scared of you is less useful than one altogether impotent or unfaithful or uninterested. The

orange toaster and dead cat put a perhaps outsized fear in me: I saw butcher knives late one night for trifling transgressions somewhere down the road. For a month we were as in love as people can be who are not altogether green, and then I was ready to go, simple as that.

Patricia understood this when I announced my unease, but she could not just accept it, so she sweetly laced her hands behind my neck and kissed me goodbye before dropping her weight and me to the floor and trying to kangaroo me. I left the Cabana to her. The Doctor would go down and rescue her with some solid girl talk and bourbon and approve of the entire affair, beginning and end. Patricia will do all right, I trust. I will see her when I see her.

•

The loose cannon in this, despite demonstrable psychological stolidity, is me, the fugitive from justice, or from cat-killing women who are your cousin, if the two are different. I would yet check into Parris Island if the forms were shorter. I swear it makes more sense than checking into Vecchio, Vecchio, and Cupola and making more buildings on our hallowed talked-to-death old ground. It would be better to fight Arabs on it, possibly better, morally, to fight Arabs on theirs, but that I honestly doubt, and do not see our letting them get here, so I will probably be an architect of some kind before a Marine of any. I regret this not joining as much as having to leave my cat-drowning, sidewalk-painting cousin, but see the pedestrian necessity in both, and see that I am finally a pedestrian, not much more. I am in something like *life*, and it is, I am afraid, not four or six or fifteen rounds once or twice or forty times, but something like a hundred thousand forgettable rounds unpunctuated by bells, unrewarded by belts, prize of contest not glory or money or domination but death. How did I get to this bright plateau so early, or at all—I once some species of child poet? Some cuddly seer of the verities, precocious prevailer? Upon all precocious prevailer the chickens of dailiness come home to roost.

Would I not be the architect born to design the fairway homes of the South? And the twenty-first century's nineteenth holes? Is that job not, by birthright, mine? At the moment this idea swelled up solid in my brain, I decided to become a commercial fisherman, sort of. And it was not fish or commerce that got me: it was paint, marine paint, how it fails virtually by definition but hangs on, gets renewed, endlessly, with an eye to some hope, some faith that it, the new coat, will hold long enough for you to take the boat out and get it back a sufficient number of times to call the endeavor, overall, successful, and for you to call yourself whatever you choose to, in this case a commercial fisherman. I had a friend from college who could build, fish, shoot, drink, womanize, fraternize, skin turtles, and thought me an egghead. He was the ideal partner for a venture predicated on a fondness for brave paint.

Jim Ball ("Do not call me Jim Balls; if my brother is with me, you may call us Balls") hesitated to venture into fishing, or anything else, with me, when I called him. His grounds, solid enough, were that I could not do anything. It was conceded I could do things inessential to the enterprise:

keep books (there'd be no money), run the office (there'd be none), write letters (to whom?). I could not pull an oil seal at sea, pull a trotline, pull a full crab pot—he did not see how I could pull my weight.

I pointed out that, despite his prowess as a West Virginian hick mountain man, *he* knew nothing about fishing beyond earthworms on a bream hook and trout spinning—they didn't even fly fish in his rude neck of the woods—and was it going to rain or not. There was more to fishing where *I* was from, I ignorant or not, than rain. He readily agreed to equivalent ignorances when it came down to locating grouper six miles out, or whatever we would locate wherever, and he liked finally the idea of besting a feeble egghead who could do not much more in life than draw it or talk about it, and I rather liked the cheer he gave off in all his bluff impatience and superiority: You can do *any*thing if you'll *do* it, his stubborn groping method said (and he *had* gotten through college without proper preparatory schooling, or measurable intelligence). So we agreed over the phone to fish for a year and see what happened. We had no money, no boat, no license, no sense. We were perfectly set up for commercial fishing.

"Where we going catch all these fish?" Jim Ball asked.

"Corpus Christi, Texas."

"Why there?"

"Never been there," I said.

"Me either. Perfect." Jim Ball had other qualities to recommend him, or derecommend him, as you prefer. He had been to Vietnam, for one thing, and interpreted

others' whims as "perfect"—deliberation or planning or rea-
sonableness was, that is, in the post-'Nam view, dumbfuck.
We agreed to meet in a week, no plans, just find each other.
We'd have been happy never finding each other, so the lack
of plan was agreeable.

13 / LEAVING PATRICIA HOD and her or-
ange rage at the Cabana, I stopped at the Grand. I needed
a kind of deep-breath, pants-hitching moment before going
on. This leaving-women thing was getting out of hand. *For
their own good*, I kept saying to myself, and half believing
it, or more than half, but having trouble not seeing the
matter from the point of view of the inexplicably abandoned.
You're some kind of cowardly lout was the competing notion, a notion that will have you pull into a place like Jake's
not a quarter mile from the abandoned woman.

So I pushed into Jake's, backwards, carrying a soup tureen found on the backseat of my car, which was no doubt
put there by my mother and which I was to have put in the
house but which I was not going to now, nor was I going
to take a Spode soup tureen to Corpus Christi, Texas. Back-
ing through the door, turning around into Jake's, I nearly
collided with a huge white man, the only one I'd ever seen
other than my old man in Jake's, who was wearing leather-
topped pull-on gumshoes and khaki pants with plough mud

all over them and who said, loudly and conspiratorially and very close to me and the tureen, "Indicted for murder!"

"Who?" I said.

"*Me.*"

I eased around him, moving the tureen away from him as you would a woman from a drunk on a dance floor. I went to the bar.

Jake was watching things very closely, sideways—his blue-jay style of close witness.

"Jake."

He took his leg down from the beer box and came toward me. I pushed the tureen to him and he took it without question and went into the back with it.

When he returned I said I wanted a cold beer made in either St. Louis or Milwaukee, not Olde English anything or Magnum anything, and two quarts of motor oil.

"Motor oil," he repeated, and again went in the back.

He presented me with a cold beer and two quarts of motor oil. "You didn't want this oil in that casserole, did you?"

"No."

The khakied drunk shouted "Call my broker!" from the front and rested his head and arms on the pinball machine by the door.

"Who'd he kill?" I asked.

"A fiddler crab," Jake said. We laughed.

"That casserole is the Doctor's. Save it for her. I've got to go. There's a crazy woman at the house."

"Know. You been shack up a month."

"Who says?"

"Lines of *communication.*"

"My great-grandfather's island!" the drunk declared, with

his head on the pinball glass and his feet now securely hung up in the rungs of the stool before the machine. He would be there for a while, it looked.

"Ain't that t.s.," Jake said.

"You want me to get him out?"

"No. We gone laugh at his ass *all night*."

"Don't hurt him."

"He *hurt*."

We laughed again. Hurt he was.

Murdering a fiddler crab was colloquial shorthand for wetlands abuse as so deemed by the various competing regulatory agencies in the low country. Red-tape fouling was so common that when an overfed man in L. L. Bean gumshoes and khaki said "Indicted for murder" and had a little mud on him and was drunk and out of place, we could put it together. On the island that his family had held since cotton and rice and indigo, the island which he now sought to make attractive at once to condominium dweller and duck hunter, the weeping man had proceeded without Coastal Council or EPA permits and, say, restored the hundred-year-old dikes which had held water for rice fields and which would now hold it for the ducks he needed to get those duck hunters to buy those condominiums, and the EPA or Coastal Council had come round and written him the equivalent of the world's largest parking ticket, say $25,000 per day per dike. He had about 2,500 feet of dike to restore to the original unrestored condition, or else, and the else meter was already running so that if he undid his dikes tomorrow he was already out $50,000, on top of the $50,000 he had spent restoring the dikes by dumping 5,000 yards of fill on them, which had inadvertently killed a fiddler crab. In his current condition, drunk in what he regarded a nigger roadhouse, he was worried that his Wild Turkey days were over; he was going to face pouring Kentucky Bourbon Deluxe into Wild Turkey bottles, to fool his friends, all the other *faux* landed gentry in the low country, and the sacred family island was going to continue being a tax liability, if the fines did not force him to have to sell it outright. He was a portrait that gave someone like Jake, whose enslaved great-grandfather had likely worked the rice paddies within the sacrosanct dikes, extreme pleasure to behold.

"Jake, were we not so close to a woman spurned, I'd like to stay and talk to you."

"About what?"

"About that fat fuck on the pinball machine."

Jake regarded this with more gravity than I would have anticipated. Then he said: "Can't live *with* 'em, Mr. Manigault, and we can't live with*out*."

I didn't want to get any deeper than that—the *Mister Manigault* was some barbedness or sarcasm too complex to have unravel in your presence. And I couldn't tell if he was referring to women or to land scions weeping in roadhouses they didn't belong in.

"I keep quitting all my girlfriends, Jake," I said. "Just up and leave."

"Can't live with them, either," he said, and laughed. "You shoot quail?"

"What?"

"Hunt birds?"

"Not regularly."

"I see."

What he saw I've no idea, but it all made sense in the

kind of charged, tacit wrestling that goes on when a black man and a white man, if I qualify, talk civilly together. You reach this kind of détente in the minuet, and when he's on your turf, he leaves, and when you're on his, you leave. I left.

•

The road out of Edisto is the best one I know to drive with nothing, or a lot, on your mind. Whether you have two quarts of oil on the seat and your arm on the window and no clear picture of a town in Texas named the Body of Christ, or you have a very clear picture of a saddened woman you've left without adequate provocation, or you have standing job interviews in Atlanta to build reflective-skin monsters or in Litchfield to build atria and wraparounds and *Southern Living* photo sets with shabbily arrogant exteriors, or you have a parent standing around foot-tapping about your failure to apply yourself as you head not to Atlanta but past it to Corpus Christi, or you have another parent in a deeper consternation about your not proving precisely *rich* in things literary to say, or you have a fat rich white man weeping about an island he owns, on a laughing black man's leased pinball machine—a tableau which involves you, too—the road out of Edisto has blasts of closeness and pastures of far-off easy silence, and smells of salt and change, or of funk and rot, and curves and straights, houses empty and black or occupied and lit, shack or brick, and you do not finally care what is on your mind or not, with all that flying by. The road out of Edisto is enough.

14 / MY FRIEND FROM COLLEGE arrived in Corpus Christi on the same day I did. We did not know this for two days, during which we each formed opinions about the unreliability of the other and about how we should go about becoming fishermen. When we met, finally, by accident, each was convinced the other was worthless and so were his ideas. My idea was to buy a big boat. Jim's idea was to buy the saltwater equivalent of a canoe, a big license, and a big truck. My idea was to *fish*, his was to *sell* fish. In this he was of course prudent. I let him have his way.

We got licenses to trade fish, and trade we did. A lot of it was standard fish wholesaling, some of it not. We got a load of shad from a game-commission netting study of some freshwater lakes and thought we could sell them. We could not sell them even to hog farmers, who told us if a hog ate a shad he would smell like a shad, not a hog, on the table. We wound up paying more money to dump the shad than we'd paid to acquire the shad.

On the whole, though, we were not unsuccessful. And that is why we did not last long. With the failures of actual fishing, I suspect we'd have been better and longer at it. But that—weather, seas, mechanical failures, monsters of the deep, charts, lights, currents—came under the heading of Romance for West Virginia Jim. "Do you think it's a *story* out there?" he'd say. "It's not a *story* out there. We sit right here on level asphalt that's not moving with a half ton of ice and wait for the fish to come to us." And that we would do, talking dully until we got the fish and hauled them to someone else becalmed on asphalt, waiting prudently for the fish, a little more expensively, to come to him. After eight months of it we divested and quit—even.

But while I was asphalt fishing in Corpus Christi something relevant occurred. My mother phoned me one night at the Cactus Motel, where for sixty dollars a week we had our corporate and private headquarters in a room with two big beds, two big windows, two big doors (front and back, the quick-exit design, though I'd stand and accept my front-door accuser before I'd have tried the gauntlet of broken glass and condoms and seagulls, dead and alive, and fan belts, and even what I think was, judging from the de-composed plastic flesh, a Judy Love Doll splayed out in that glass, etc., as if awaiting your fall into her arms, her ruby rubbery O-shaped mouth suggesting surprise until you realized what it really suggested and gingerly stepped back into your sixty-dollar room, the evening con-stitutional over)—she phoned and the office manager came down and got me and I went to the office and as I began speaking with her, just as I began realizing she might be drinking, the office manager said to me, "Would you please get *off the pone.*"

I looked at him quizzically.

"It's a business *pone*," he said, with great conviction and certainty. That I could not deny. Figuring the logic of his giving me the business pone not two minutes before taking it back was beyond me, beyond anybody; what occupied me, besides trying to hear my mother, was whether the office manager had any teeth. You never *saw* them, yet his face was not collapsed either. I said to him, inspired: "Go get the tequila from my room, limes in the sink. I know goddamn well this is a goddamn business pone."

"Who's that?" my mother was saying, I imagine—I was watching my man petulantly, but not altogether reluctantly, leave the little office.

"I'm back," I said to her, when I could, and she was in mid-sentence carrying on, and I had to start trotting along with her to get up to speed. A locating word was "Father." Then "not too upset," which I at first took to apply to Patricia Hod but then took to refer to the old man, logical in all ways. Patricia Hod would be either *not* upset or, if upset, would have burnt the house down, and my father was perpetually not *too* upset. One more hard locator item and I'd have her, my mother, triangulated without having to slow her down. The manager came back in, solemnly carrying the bottle and the limes, put them down defiantly on the desk, and glared at me. I held up two fingers and made a little circular motion, and he raised his eyebrows, to which I circled some more and gave the two fingers again, and he bent slightly and pulled up, from behind the desk as if it were a miniature bar, two glasses. With one hand I unscrewed the tequila and poured the glasses full and set the bottle down hard. "I know goddamn well this is a goddamn business pone," I said again.

"*Am I saying anything?*" he shouted, picking up his drink.

"—because you haven't contact—" my mother was saying—"con*tact*ed those . . ."

"Mother, you mean the jobs?"

"The po*sit*ions." She was drunk, furious. What was bubbling up here in these emphases was her unending disappointment that I was, apparently, even in *not* contacting my po*sit*ions, an architect—that my father had prevailed. For this she was not angry at me, as she should have been, but at him, which was easier and which preserved hope: it was not me who had not become the William Wordsworth of Wadmalaw, it was he, my old man, who had stopped me. I could yet be salvaged. I was not altogether *manqué*, simply not yet found. She was seething. I chuckled, toasting, as I did, the manager, who solemnly returned the gesture, with a shooing of his free hand telling me to go ahead, keep talking, using the business pone.

"What's so *funny?*" my mother asked.

"Nothing."

"You'd better . . ."

"I'd better what?"

"Stop that."

"Stop what?"

"Stop . . . *everything*."

At this, despite myself, I laughed again. It was not a prudent move, but it could not be helped. Before I could repair the damage, sure enough, she hung up. I looked, as one will, at the mouthpiece of the phone and held it in the air regarding it long enough for the manager to understand I'd been hung up on.

He shrugged. "Your girl?"

"Yeah."

"I don't like Saturdays worth a damn. Everybody don't like Monday, but I do. Saturday is a bunch of hooey."

I poured us some more tequila, had him get us some salt, and we drank a few little shots, looking out at traffic and not saying much. I could not figure out, drink in and drink out, watching him at all furtive angle and even watching him bite limes, if he had teeth or not.

In the little office, with its pine paneling and bad carpet and out-of-date calendars on the wall, the business pone idle, all the cars going by, I thought to think the moment one of contentment, a kind of contentment likely not to be enjoyed forever. That is an odd emotion, drinking with a geezer and with a Judy Love Doll out the back door of your room, but it is an emotion that is true.

"You know what else is not all it's cracked up to be?" I asked the manager.

"What?"

"Fishing."

"That shit," he said, "is for *the birds*."

We both laughed, fine fast friends if there ever were fine fast friends in this world. I think I saw a tooth.

"Fishing *on a Saturday* about the worst idea in the world," he said.

15 / THE WAY WE had worked it, fishing *any* day was, to my mind, the worst idea in the world. We didn't spot a school of fish and lower lines or nets, we spotted a good price on a case of thirty-weight and pulled into AutoZone and debated whether we needed fan belts and oil or just oil. I got thoroughly impatient with the enterprise, though we were making money. Not a lot, but enough to be surprised when we looked at the checkbook.

We pulled into a wholesaler's one day and saw some Vietnamese standing about the lot in positions of consternation, itself a sign that something wasn't right. You saw Vietnamese working or you did not see them. If they were talking, moreover standing around and talking, there was an obstacle in their path. I didn't want any part of it.

"This looks like Vietnam," I said to Jim, driving. "Westmoreland's inside, weighing three hundred pounds, tahkin like iss, refusing to sell them something or buy something from them, playing with his hairy gut through the side ports of his overalls, wondering why in hail we *din't* bomb them into the Stone Age, *why?* Theron, I ast you, *why?*" I was, as I say, impatient with the entire affair.

"What you know about Vietnam wouldn't form a good dingleberry in your BVDs," Jim said, as expected. I was in for the harangue: HE HAD BEEN. I had not.

"Let me see if I can get it right, Jim. We know who went, *but we don't know who came back.* Is that it? Do I have it right?"

"Fuck you."

"Fine with me."

This was fishing on asphalt. I got out of the van to go in to find Haystacks Calhoun Westmoreland and buy something, but as I neared the Vietnamese I heard them speaking English first and switch to French, and that did it. That did it. I went up to the van window and said to Jim, "They doing French, *mon cher*, to elude me. When I let them know I speak it, they'll switch to something else."

"Gook. Gook's hard." He laughed.

I waved agreeably at the Vietnamese and said across the lot, *"Laisse le bon temps roulé,"* which confused them, understandably, but they knew it *meant* to be French, and when I went back by them, sure enough, they were speaking something that sounded like Hungarian.

•

I went in and found the proprietor. I took one look at him and left. He *was* in overalls, and white Red Ball boots, slopping around—ahhch, I'd had it.

"Take me to the suite," I told Jim. "I quit."

"Bullshit."

"No. I'm not talking to one more Klansman in rubber boots, ever. Won't do it."

"I'll do it."

"You do it."

I got to the Cactus Motel and walked a good long hot walk down to the liquor store and got a generous stock of stuff I felt appropriate to celebrating the end of my post-college dalliance. On the way back I threw away a beer can in an oil drum and saw on top of the trash in the can a large, colorful, lifelike dildo. It had a tube running from it to a squeeze bulb of the sort you see on certain pneumatic toys. I stood there regarding it agreeably for a long time, amazed by its veins and knurls and hues, and thought to myself that if I *were* an artist, I was having an epiphany. I've had an epiphany, I said to myself walking back to the Cactus, kicking smashed beer cans and marveling at the proximity of the dildo to the Judy Love Doll out the back door. So close, so far. If wedded, what beautiful music they might make. I was a man of uncertain future afraid to pick up an abandoned dildo and give it to an abandoned deflated woman. I think I saw a small snake in the grass of the road shoulder, and if I did, it looked considerably less real, or less probable, or more outlandish than did the dildo in the garbage. Everybody in the world, granting a certain statistical exception, knows what he's doing, except me, was my next thought. This was at once of course ludicrously untrue and vigorously sound, and I liked it. It gave comfort, especially if I could eliminate the statistical exceptions and have it *really* be true. If the plastic woman through her scarlet O-ring mouth were calling siren-fashion the lost dildo to her, it made no less sense than did my life. I had once been rational, as a child. That time looked as far away and as probable as Jules Verne's Lost Island.

16 / AND SO I QUIT TEXAS, where I had gone, I confess, for imprudent reasons. The Doctor had had me read, of course, all Faulkner, and if you take nothing else from him, which is prudent, you may remember that he designates Texas as where you go and change your name when your schemes don't work out. These are the kind of schemes which when they do work out everybody says you're smart and you remain in Mississippi or Virginia or South Carolina or even Oglethorpian Georgia—honorable (the Wawer, the Wawer) next to Texas, a place too low for the Snopeses! I had had to see it for myself, albeit in an homogenized latter-day state, its dastardly modern equivalent to horse thieves represented by million-dollar attorneys so removed from horses they nickname themselves Racehorse. Lyndon Johnson was conceivably the model prototypical outlaw by the time I got to old change-your-name Texas. I suppose at the other end of the spectrum it was the Klansmen in rubber boots who schemed for a while to have commercial fishing all to themselves, whose scheme was not working out precisely because the scheme—and was this not Mr. Johnson's scheme finally?—to bomb Vietnam into the Stone Age had not worked out. In a way Texas was a great epicenter of the not-working-out, and I should have loved it, but I did not.

Their pride *in pride* is oppressive, cheerless, unlaughable. Something in you wants to film it, but something else wants a robot to run the camera for you while you . . . change your name and go somewhere else.

So Texas I abandoned, the prospect of being a historically in-tune, enviro-friendly, twill-clad, post-and-beam architect no longer troublesome. That's what I thought to do, so in Atlanta I stopped to interview with the *other* guys, in order to decline the opportunity to join them and be a historically out-of-tune, enviro-blind, twill-clad, skin-and-skeleton architect. The interview was thorough. Four of the not senior fellows took me out, they could drink, we wound up after hours looking for an open club, we found one, it was gay, we ordered up, and I am greeted heartily by the General— the president of the small college in which my mother teaches.

He says, taking me by the shoulder as if to lead me somewhere and show me off, "Whoa! Whoa! I didn't *know!*" He's the picture of mirth—country-club camaraderie and thigh-slapping. What on earth do you make of this earth? A man who has hounded friends of my mother out of jobs for their alleged homosexuality—on the strength of seeing me, recognizing me from not much more than a few conversations with my mother, with me at her side, years ago—feeling me, kneading me, steering me through a hundred leering, winking guys who know a bit more than I do, it would seem, about him. I start laughing and find no way not to go along with the General's presumptions and gumption. There are raised eyebrows at the bar where my interviewers are suspended, not yet tasting their drinks, wondering now how good an idea coming with hot young prospect Simons Manigault into a place called the Golden Flame was.

17 / THERE, IN A GAY BAR, at one in the morning, being watched by my red-blooded interviewers with their eyebrows irrepressibly raised as the college president for whom my mother teaches paws me, I have a vision of sorts. It is of the lover of my mother whom I called Taurus, who was ostensibly not a white man altogether, who went apparently to Louisiana when he was done with my mother or when she was done with him. I have left enough women to know that the matter is never clear: even if one party drops off the key, Lee, and the other merely weeps, there has been some crossfire, however muted, and there has been some leveraging out on the part of the left. But at one in the morning in the Golden Flame, I see only my man Taurus, sitting in a bar, a different kind of bar, with knotty paneling and room for only ten or so serious fools, in Louisiana, with a bright yellow fizzing beer in a six-ounce straight glass and an expression on his face that is inscrutable. And I am going to Louisiana. Where I have no business, but I have no business with the General's ham-sized paw kneading my shoulder and forcing me, eventually, to

go back to my escorts and feign sheepishness and explain this. No. When I get this vision of Taurus, a man singular in the long unsingular run of suitors to my own mother, I have the courage to walk back to the T-square technicians who call themselves artists and ask, "Gentlemen, you fellows ever tried the true stuff?" They freeze—not able even to blush, let alone snort. "Until you do, it cannot be explained."

I know it will be explained at the office the next morning, in high hilarity and close-call head-shaking sighs. Their discomfort is marginally amusing. Not amusing enough. The General, in his large, loose presumption, is better company than this small, tight presumption of the professionally-taking-itself-seriously.

I spend a night in a giant glass tower of the sort they would have me draw for a living and observe from my window, at intervals, the construction of a receiving awning and the cordoning off of a two-block area by a profusion of at least three kinds of police. Checking out the next morning, I learn that the President is coming for a stay. May he be gay, too.

I stop around the corner at a liquor store—I do not mean to go into Louisiana unarmed—and witness what I take to be a scene, but the players don't apparently regard it as much. A black man stumbles into the store and is denied a purchase—I miss whether he has no money or whether he has been deemed too drunk to buy more booze. As this denial obtains in his brain, he begins to huff and rumble, finally managing something like, directed at the black clerk, "Fuck you *up*." The clerk says, "Go on."

"Bsht!" A stagger and a wave that is then, from its

momentum only, known to have been a swing at the clerk.

"Get out of here."

"Fuck you *up!*"

"I'mone tear *you* up, nigger," the clerk says, untying his apron.

That does it. The denied eases out, bumping from jamb to jamb, and the store is back to business as usual. I notice that I am the only customer among five who is white and who has been holding his breath. The others have formed a line ahead of me with their purchases, impatient. I watch the clerk scrupulously to see if he regards me or my transaction any differently from the others, and he does not. Where I come from there would have been apology or dismissal, explanation or gesture made to accommodate me, to persuade me the drunk and the vulgarity were exceptional. Or during the fracas, the clerk might say "Buckra heah." Here, no. Atlanta is on its own, I take it, racially, and it is the only thing I witness in it that argues I stay. But I do not stay: they are already goosing each other about me in the suites of Eco, Ergo and Ague, and I am going to Louisiana with a banjo on my knee.

Do I expect to find this man? Why, excepting that it is absurd to do so, should I not? Have I not seen my careerist peers panicked by prospect of homosexual contagion, my non-careerist non-peers not panicked by prospect of physical violence, my President panicked by prospect of assassination, when all he wants is a quiet room at the Omni? Is it more absurd to think to find one mysterious man who, as I recall him, was not panicked by anything, in half a million panicked men in Louisiana? Not absurd enough.

I drive a long time. If you prefer old federal highways that are drained of blood by parallel interstates, they are happily drained also of asphalt, and you click and clunk and click down them slowly enough to study the shells and hulls of cinder-block motels and bars clinging to them like cicada husks to moribund trees. I wind up in desolate region in desolate hour, with no motel in sight, and then finally there is one. The breath I hold against No Vacancy turns out to be fanciful when the clerk, a black woman, chuckles, "Sure there's room," and I wish immediately maybe there had not been. There are about ten rooms, with most of the doors open at one in the morning and couples in them managing to look at me, led by my key to No. 8. They are all black. The looks are *bothered*, not uncivil, but containing curiosity run over quickly by resentment. Resenting what, I no longer am naïve enough to wonder. Nor do I wonder how I graduate from the black liquor store and its business to this black whorehouse (as near as I can hazard) with its business— you get in grooves in life, and you by God stay in them until the record plays out. So be it. What I do wonder is why so many doors are open for them to see me, as if each couple is expecting more company, if it is actually couples in the rooms (you have, with your circumspect glance as you watch ostensibly your own feet, time to see only a drink or a bottle, a man or a woman, a hand, a look, an earring, a mustache, another look). I close the door to my room. A card on the table says "Latesha," like that, in quotes, and then, also in quotes, a phone number.

I call my mother. She's asleep. Otherwise she would not cooperate.

"Mother."

"Son."

"That man I called Taurus, your . . ."

"My friend."

"Yes. Where is he?"

"Where *is* he?"

"Yes." I expect her to disclaim, fight, dodge, vituper possibly. The interview of one's mother on the subject of her lovers is not indelicate. My timing—her being nine-parts asleep (agreeable) and one part her true self—allows purchase.

"Where he is, oh. He's . . . you *did* call him Taurus." She giggles.

"You all let me."

"If you'd called him Aquarius, we'd have stopped that." She outright laughs, as if this is much funnier than it is: she is laughing at something else. What, I can't fathom, and it may have to do with how much (or little—this, too, you never know) she's had to drink tonight.

"Well, where is this raging bull, Mother?"

"That's a laidlow to—"

"No, Mother, it's not. It's a question."

I swear to God I hear all the motel doors close and the couples are already moaning. Black sexual moaning sounds like white medical trauma. There is a back room at the Grand I spent some childhood under. "It's a question, Mother. I want to know where Taurus, stud, is."

"He's a game warden in Ville Platte, Louisiana."

"How did I know he was in Louisiana?"

"Honey, I hardly know how *I* know he's in Louisiana."

"He's a *game warden*?"

"He's straddling law and law en*force*ment," she says. "That's his . . . game."

"I see."

"No, you don't."

"I don't?"

"No."

"Why?"

"Because you *think* you're smart, but you're people dumb."

"I'm people dumb?"

"Eat up with it."

"He's *your* ex-lover, not mine," I say, wild. There are knocking sounds in deep muffle through the wall to No. 9, into which I did not get a glimpse. I move away from the wall, looking at the floor, expecting to see something leaking through. I get the creeps, but I'm in a domestic engagement. My mother is pulling a partial rear enfilade on the phone. "Your lover grandson to your stroked-out maid, Mother, if I recall correctly."

"People dumb," she says, and there is a sound with it that suggests she may be crying, and I hang up. I am crying, too. May the world excuse me. I will not cry over, or with, or for my mother again.

People dumb. She's right, of course. But what a brutal thing to say. If nothing else, I can live and die and say when it is over, Yes, I came to nothing, but my mother, my mother was a pro.

18 / LOUISIANA WAS a tunnel of improbability. For starters, I could not stop drinking. This, I know, is statistically not improbable if you are bred for it, if you have in your soul the Mendelian, green, wrinkled pea for booze, and I indubitably do, but I had never felt the real pull of it before. Booze has been for me recreation, sideboard theater, camp, a headache. Occasionally, insupportable behavior. Occasionally, magical moments.

But crossing into Louisiana I got this haunted little rill of feeling—there was moss and mud everywhere and an inexplicable, hollow sensation that Louisiana is what would be left of the South after it has been nuked—that I and everything around me were irretrievably rotten. I was passing through this rotten-looking, rotten-sounding town called Slidell and I got some crayfish and ate them with mustard. Pygmy lobsters from the swamp and Zatarain's mustard from the jar and some kind of sharp whiskey from the bottle, which had the effect of Cowper's fluid on the crustaceans and mustard going down; I could swear the little things were snapping their tails in what felt like gasoline in my throat, and I felt so bad and out of it—no job, no friends, no Henry Miller—that I felt very, very, very good. I felt like boxing a few rounds with . . . with live oaks. I felt like driving. And that I did. Somewhere right at the beginning I stopped and asked someone, "Is this Slidell?" and before he could answer yelled, "*I* am Slidell," and drove very slowly away, waving and smiling a huge exaggerated smile at him, or her, it may have been a dog.

I wanted to be black and named Slidell Washington. I had whiskey. I passed Mandeville, which I knew somehow was the premier state nuthouse, and stepped on it hard. I came to in a bar.

There, relatively calm, I realized Mandeville was maybe where they shanghaied Earl Long, but I was too near it yet and scared by being Slidell Washington to ask anyone. If I were black and asked about Mandeville and Earl Long they would just put me *in* Mandeville. I had a drink before me on the bar, and there was a very attractive unattractive lifer barmaid smoking down the way who had served me the drink, apparently. I went to the bathroom to see if I was black, and was not. I washed my face anyway, convinced I was. I didn't mind that actually—the idea of being *secretly* black was agreeable. But I didn't want anyone finding out, or finding out suddenly and scaring everyone and me, too. This is where a drink works like an oar on a boat in a moving current. You have one, you need another to row, to control, because shit is happening.

I went out to the bar, sat down to address my drink, and a very loud noise occurred. And apparently only I heard it.

When I got up out of the crouch I was in beside my stool, the bartender was looking at me.

"You okay?" she said.

I knew immediately she had not heard the noise. She could not possibly have heard it and still be upright, smoking. But I had to say, anyway, "You didn't hear that?"

"Hear what?"

"That, ah, explosion?"

She just looked at me. I had enough instinct still to know if I said one more word I'd not get one more drink from her.

"Sorry, ma'am. Flashback city."

She was not reassured by this, because I do not look flashback qualified, unless we are talking drug flashback, but I averted crossing the cutoff line, and I drank the drink before me and got another as quickly as I could and tipped her well right then, with more money visible on the bar— that wordless, grave tipping you do by pushing the money solemnly at them, interrupting their retreat, even touching her hand if you're really up to something other than ensuring service during your first serious drunk. I was swimming in ordure. I was having promiscuous thoughts—not ribald thoughts, but thoughts that were changing among themselves in a blurred and indiscriminate fashion. I was drunk and it felt good in a way I knew was not good. I had the wit to keep all this to myself and keep getting drinks and never figured out the huge noise. From matchbooks I figured out I was in Covington, probably.

I had a scratch on my arm and didn't know how I'd scratched it. The noise I'd heard seemed to be coming from it, a little at a time. I looked to the woman to see if she heard *that.* She mistook my glance for a ready sign and made me a drink. Whatever she was making me had changed color. My arm was now speaking.

It said, "Shut up."

"Okay," I said to it.

"You're welcome," the bartender said.

"Your mother," my arm said.

I waited for more. "My mother what?"

"I don't know," it said.

I looked at the scratch closely. I wanted to see its lips move if I could. I put my head on my arm, level with the forest of hairs, the wild terrain of follicle and freckle and fleshy soil, waiting for this fresh fault in the land to speak. I bit myself, at first rather affectionately, then shook my arm like a bulldog a rag and made noises. "Your mother's on the phone," it said. I dropped my arm.

"What?"

The bartender was over us. "Your mother—she says—is on the phone."

"My *mother* is on the phone?"

"That's what she says. It's a woman. You called her, I think. Before."

That is as close to a summary position on the evils of drink as I can imagine: Don't drink, because if you do and it gets off the road with you, you can be invited to speak to your mother in a bar you do not know the location of on a phone it is alleged, but you do not remember, you have used. It is like a call to armed combat when you are unaware you're in the service. *Flat feet* understates the matter; 4-F will not at this hour suffice. You trudge, you limp, you lollygag to the phone, and, with a look and high sign for a drink to the bartender, who's rather your commanding officer at the moment, you pick up the phone.

"I did it," she says.

"Did what?"

"Called him."

"Who?"

"What's with you, Son?"

"Nothing's with me."

"Something's with you."

"Ty-D-Bol."

"What?"

"Nothing."

"O.K. Bar Number Two, Mamou."

"Tokyo tumbler egg foo, to you."

"Son, you asked me to find him, I did."

I had no idea—well, *some* idea, but wasn't happy about my disadvantages. The best thing to do was bluff, so I got her to repeat the information and got off the phone. It was a wall phone and somehow I nearly fell down hanging up, and would have had I missed the cradle. I straightened up and did not feel as drunk as I had, and I had a reasonable guess that this information regarded the man-myth Taurus, and that I'd called my mother during the deep passion storm of the early rising part of the drunk. I was in the late used-rag part now, where passion is an old fond friend you wish well. You trust he's well but would be content never to see him again. But here I'd gone and *made a date* during the friskies. Mamou.

I sat back down and the bartender came over with a drink

and swept the money out of the way and leaned over the
bar with both arms—as if to straighten my tie, which I was
not wearing—her hands coming in tenderly and slowly at
my throat and sliding around my neck and lacing behind
it, and she pulled me to her, hard, and kissed me, hard, full
on the mouth, and turned her head forty-five degrees, serious. It was done with such energy I gave her energy back,
and tried to give back what seemed the spirit of the thing.
It's just *a kiss*, do it *well*, she seemed to be saying. She
let me go and I rocked back down on the four legs of the
stool.

"Not bad," she said.

"No," I said.

She went back to her station and didn't regard me much
after that; some regulars came in and I knew we were
over. It was an agreeable affair. Her hair—I grabbed her
neck, too—was like bleached hemp, almost as coarse and
stiff as shredded wheat, and felt very sturdy and good to
the hands but nothing like hair. People were calling her
Dotty.

By way of saying goodbye, I told her, over some of the
regulars, which made me look nuttier than anything I'd
done in there yet, I think, "Hey, Dotty, I've got to *go*. I've
got a *dog* to feed." It was as if I were Admiral Byrd saying,
"Hey, I've got to go. I've got a *pole* to claim." I said this to
a group of explorers who had not yet begun their journeys.
The entire bar paused and did a very discreet but palpable
eye roll, except Dotty, who managed, unseen by anyone, to
wink at me. It was the wink of one-kiss lovers, a salutation
across all time between two people forever in love who had

strained to do something mystifying to each other across a countertop. "Well," I said when the eye roll had completed itself and I felt they were all embarrassed to have presumed Dotty would join them, and I wanted to say Hi-yo, Silver! as well, but did not, and left.

Outside, the mud and gloom had changed to something radically more Hallmark: it was all bright bayou and butterflies. At my car I had a shock: I *did* have a dog. There was a robust, gnashing Dalmatian in my car. There was a glimmer of history about this dog, which I sought to mollify with some *Easy, boy,* which he was having none of. St. Tammany Parish Animal Control Center. Had stopped thereat. Why? Because had stopped at Tulane Primate Research Center. Why? To see monkeys with wires coming out of their heads. Was not allowed to. Why? Probably because they had monkeys with monkeys coming out of their heads, which is why primate research centers are in swamps. This had pissed me off, so I stopped at dog pound down road to see what abuse *they* were up to. Not an animal nut, but even the name Primate Research Center gives me willies. So whip in dog pound, and first dog run has Dalmatian nearly breaks through chain-link to get me. This I remember vividly, standing now at my car wondering how to get in it: this very dog hitting the fence with force enough to bulge it in rhomboids of fur and bounce back, squinting very meanly and sideways at me, growl almost inaudible, saliva on galvanized wire.

"That ain't no fire-station dog out there," I said inside the place with some old-boy gusto and sawmill conviction, and a fellow chuckled, No, it ain't, it was the pound guard dog, though, and I said I wanted it, and evidently I got it. I had got bad drunk and got a bad dog and called my bad mother and made a date to meet one of her bad lovers. I had torn a page, I believe the locution goes. All I could do now was buy some meat across the street and throw it in the backseat and drive and hope the dog did not bite me in the back of the head. I had gotten him *in* the car; it looked marginally tenable he'd let me in it now.

He did and we drove off. I named him My Inner Life. At the first pee stop My Inner Life ran off down a logging canal on a bayou named, as near as I can tell, Tennessee Williams. If it was not Tennessee Williams it was Joe Bourgeois, my map was considerably out of register. Up this same canal down which My Inner Life had disappeared shortly came loping toward me a giant nutria, bounding part beaver, part rat, with yellow incisors visible like a nine ball in its mouth. I could not get Louisiana. Huey Long and open-skulled monkeys and logging canals and South American rodents gamboling the land, and that land a weird admixture of ordinary South—landscaped colonial brick Farmers & Merchants Banks at crossroads where there appears no need for a bank, or for a crossroads, or for roads, and no farms are about—and unordinary South. The unordinary obtained when you found a canal named for a man named Joe Bourgeois or Tennessee Williams, take your pick. This canal here, in this swamp we ruined pulling oil out of it, and pulling logs out of it before that, let's name it for John Doe—no, for that guy (queer, I think) who made that streetcar of ours, which no longer runs, I think, famous. Yes. Need him a canal. Somewhere out in the vast swamp before me could be an intersection of forgotten waterways called Dealey Plaza and Garrison Slough. I ran, a little ahead of the nutria, back to my car. There I found a receipt that indicated My Inner Life had had all his shots and was worm free and had cost forty-five dollars.

19 / AT A JOINT CALLED the O.K. Bar No. 2 outside Mamou, I waited for my mother's old lover, I think. I think it was the No. 2—perhaps I was in one of a chain of rough Cajun roadhouses (there was a great iron pan of crayfish for everyone, and I had some and was a stranger to no one's discomfort)—and I think I waited for him, though it is possible he had been waiting for me, so smoothly and unceremoniously did he slide into the chair opposite me at some point. I had the feeling he'd been watching me.

There was immediately none of the big-brother directness, frontal elderliness, that I recall from our time before, but instead a kind of diffidence. He did not look so much at me as at the table between us, a little landscape of the lost lousy life: crayfish heads and beer in puddles. He put a crayfish head on his finger and moved it slightly, puppetlike.

"You've changed, but not much," he said, and we both watched the crayfish on his finger as if it were the speaker.

It was fine with me if it were. I had the sudden conviction there were plenty of things I did not want to know about this man. They were things that would disappoint me in my heroic memory of him as suitor to my mother, superior to Odysseus, as mentor to me, superior to Mentor.

He was smaller than I'd thought, but it was the knotted-down, dangerous-looking smallness of frame that you do not fuck with. And this looking-at-the-table business did not seem to indicate shyness so much as don't fuck with me. I couldn't think of a damned thing to say.

So we sat there. I thought we were like a couple of guys who'd get on better in the presence of women, but that meant one of them would be, in the likely neighborhood of our short history, my mother, and that didn't seem to be the kind of thing I had in mind. I couldn't get a fix on his age. He was in a flannel shirt. His hands were worked, thumbs suggesting small lobster claws. My hands were, and are, women's hands, approximately.

"Come on," he said.

He stopped at a glass cooler by the bar and removed two six-packs of beer from it and did not wait for acknowledgment from anyone, just left. *I* looked around to ratify this purchase, if it was one, and no one paid me any mind. His truck was moving when I got in it. "Better get your car," he said, and I did that and followed him.

We went somewhere and somewhere else and somewhere and somewhere else, as if I were being kidnapped blindfolded. I had no idea where we were when we stopped and parked in a limestone cul-de-sac, the graded stone road looking phosphorescent in the moonlight, and got in a pirogue. It had a small forward deck on which was a dead nutria. As we motored the canal of some sort, I mezzed out on this nutria. Its tail was the size of a giant carrot and it had a dusky finely wrinkled skin like the callus on an old dog's elbow, but it had hair coming out of it like fine stiff black wire. Or like the fiber inside moss, the dried core they used to stuff furniture with that you virtually cannot break. We went a long way on this canal, or these canals, or whatever they were, with the same you-might-as-well-be-blindfolded sense obtaining. I thought I might as well relax.

Life itself was, as I had been leading it, a blindfolded—volitionally in my case—affair. Were I not seeking the blindfold I'd have been already working in Atlanta or having a brotherly man-to-man with my father over some fine point in the management of my Republican portfolio. I was in a plywood boat with a giant dead rodent leading the darkly way. In the old days you got by Cerberus, the three-headed dog. Today you got by Nutria, the one-headed rat. Charon was a man who didn't speak, didn't look at you, slept with your mother, you thought, you hoped, once, but now you wondered what kind of queer desire it was to hope a man, any man other than your father—no, *including* your father—had slept with your mother. Who *should* sleep with your mother? Should anyone? The answer, in a bayou with barred owl accompanying us head-high in the tupelo gums and a hint of goner funk coming off the just-stiff nutria bowsprit, seemed to be *no*. No one should sleep with your mother. Ever. This would eliminate you and your problems.

I got a beer and enjoyed the ride. I saw a moccasin the size of a fat Schwinn tire, his white eye band bright off the water like a big smile. And I'm sure he was smiling: we were all out there in a moon-bright bayou, lost souls smiling in our lostness, the dead nutria the most content, but all of us having a very good time. This is what bayou and beer and lovers of your mother will have you believe, at night. In the daytime, of course, yanh yanh yanh . . .

20 / WE GOT TO A HOUSE on stilts in a row of houses on stilts, a Main Street, of sorts, of black water. Access to this little town was decidedly by boat, or helicopter, if that wouldn't blow the houses down, and it looked as if it would. Ours was two stories high, but the first story was stilts and the building itself was only seven feet floor to ceiling and, like the pirogue, seemed made entirely of plywood. Then I noticed parts of it were cardboard and other parts rusted-out screen. It fairly thundered when we walked in, and bent and gave, trampoline-like. It had a refrigerator that looked about fifty years old, with thick round ivory shoulders, about the size and bulk of a safe. A yellow bug light came on inside it when opened, and I noticed all the lights in the house, and, later, in the town itself, were yellow.

Taurus, if that was to be his name again, let me take it in and said, "Some nurses are coming by in a bit."

"What?"

"Nurses."

"Nurses?"

"Yes." He went into a small room and left me with this prospect. Did he mean nurses in a figurative sense, in which case they could be outright whores as long as they cured you, and in which case he was joking as well as my father and his clan might joke, or did he mean it literally? You could only hope he meant *nurses*. I was in the epicenter of a time and place where no questions should be asked, or thought I was, not unreminiscent of the times I'd had with this man before, when things were so obscure and adult around me and him that I chose to be a kind of passive radio receiver of the signals of enigma swirling around. He came back through to the yellow-blaring refrigerator, and I toyed with the radio philosophy a bit: "What for?"

"What what for?"

"The nurses."

"Health."

There you go. Answers to questions in these radio-silence zones of human endeavor constitute diminishing returns. Do not ask. Prepare for nurses. How to prepare for nurses? Get a beer. Get sick. Lie down. Look feeble.

I did all this, feeling fine on a kind of bamboo sofa over-looking the bayou, or whatever we'd come in on, the town's twenty or so pirogues sticking out into it like teeth from a comb, I with no idea if this town was for fishing or receiving nurses or pursuing nutria or what. But this was "out there," and it felt good, not unlike I used to feel as a child in our house on the Atlantic, which by now was al-together suburban. There were some flies on their backs on the windowsill, quaintly dead. A pirogue motored along and paused, and a man took the nutria off the bow of ours and put it on the bow of his and motored on with the same want of circumspection Taurus had used taking the beer in the bar. It was dark, but the man appeared to be made of rust.

"Small problem," Taurus called from the room he'd gone into again. "Yours is large. But young."

"Young?"

"Under thirty."

"Large?"

"Under three hundred."

Oh, Patricia. I had had Patricia Hod, who might have been crazy but who was a marvelous woman otherwise, and now I had . . . what? I had trouble, I had waste, I had misery a-comin' and I did not look forward to it. I lay there like Cleopatra on my divan, waiting for a date on this little tannin-colored Nile. I got ravenous. Three hundred pounds would not be enough. This entire place and setting and setup was so squalid it began to blossom with bright, false possibility: we were flowers, us humans, of infinite variety and stripe and hope, each of us perfumed with our unique potential.

Then I saw two women tromping down the shore, both in white, both nurses indubitably, and the one following the first was indeed as broad and squat as the little Philco refrigerator.

Taurus was over and behind me, looking. "You can call her Sweetie or Catfish," he said. Just as they came up the stairs he added, "Be careful."

"Why?"

"She's the daughter."

In the brief time we all spent together that followed, I saw that what he meant was *he* had to be careful. The mother, whom he called Mrs. Ames, watched the daughter with a kind of indifferent scrutiny that suggested at once a father watching a son, hoping he'd get laid, and a mother watching a daughter to see that she did not. By "Be careful" Taurus had instructed me to slip between the zones of this paternal-maternal coverage. I had to be interested in Sweetie but not aggressive; I had to let her come on to me when she did, and prompt her to when she did not. This was difficult with a large, strange woman you did not want.

We all had some beer together, during which time Mrs. Ames talked about work, its headaches, and Sweetie confirmed her sentiments. Mrs. Ames suggested that Sweetie and I go down to the water. There I screwed my courage into one sweet ball and kissed her, as her silent, vaguely impatient, moon-gazing planting of herself on a small dock suggested she wanted, or expected. She had bumpy skin, some kind of unexpressed acne, not unlike the shaving bumps on black guys. She was inert, but still seemed impatient, so I touched one of her breasts, which could not have fit into a bucket. She remained inert, or impatient, I was distracted by her size at this point, and I pressed and lifted the breast up, which required subtly getting under it with a little shoulder. At this she pushed me back and said, with great practiced authority one might use on a horse, "Hold on, Junior."

"What?"

"I said *Hold on*, Junior."

"No problem." I held her lamely a minute more about the waist and then politely disengaged—sensing she expected me to continue my assault—and had no more to do with her. I looked at the stars and she looked at the water and I hoped Taurus knew he had about three minutes to effect his exchange with Mrs. Ames, mother of Catfish, before I left Catfish on the bayou and got on that divan thing and went to sleep.

·

I woke up cold, with the feeling the house was resettling itself, as if Mrs. Ames and Catfish had just tromped out of it, adjusting their purses on their shoulders, and were to be seen in parade going back up the foggy bayou whence they'd come, and I was about to look when Taurus, sitting at a table in the center of the room, said, "Your mother wanted you to be great. But she really wanted to be great herself."

"I know that."

"Women do this. Men don't give a damn."

"What stopped her?"

"From being great?"

"Yeah."

"You."

"Right."

"In her heart, she thinks that, probably. Not bitterly and not often."

"I believe you."

This conversation did not strike me as odd at the time. I did not ponder how he knew or presumed to know these things, or why he was uncharacteristically, according to my memory of him, spouting like this. It all seemed rather natural, if not necessary, in the Hiroshima wake of the Ames sex bombing and I guess in the entire business of my presuming and managing to find him. Who was he for me to find, who was I to find him, who was my mother to be his lover? In all the not knowing, it seemed a little speculation was called for, not simply excusable.

"She has the passion to believe that," he said, "and to believe in something like being great, whatever it means. Men don't give a shit, more and more. If they ever did."

"What do you mean?"

"In olden days when there was . . . opportunity, you could be Caesar. Now . . ."

"Now we are at best amateurs at seizing opportunity. These are my very words."

"What?"

"Nothing. What about you?"

"What *about* me?"

"She thought you were great, I take it. You seized *something*. Albeit my own mother—"

"She mistook me for you, for a minute, and for your old man, for a minute longer, and then saw I was neither and let me go. She saw I was nothing."

"What are you?"

"I'll tell you what I should have been. I should have been a wild-haired Hungarian that made the atomic bomb or one rough buck nigger. I'm a game warden. I don't hunt. I hunt men who hunt. I hunt them inexactly."

"Guy came by got that nutria."

"I see."

"He supposed to?"

"He supposed to."

This moment evoked completely and perfectly what I remembered of my earlier time with this man. He left, into his little room.

21 / IN THE MORNING we had some meat I was convinced was breakfast nutria and got two umbrellas that had Notre Dame printed on them and motored away in the pirogue. I was utterly turned around, if I'd ever been oriented. It was raining, hard, yet with promise of doing it all day, and you soon wondered what sense it made being in a boat as opposed to just wading or swimming. We went through miles of stumped swamp and duckweed and tortured stands of tupelo gums with their skirts up, showing their roots. I saw no animals. Then I saw what looked like a Mexican in a small clearing. He had a pirogue—as regular as a Chevrolet out here—and watched us, casually, pass.

"What's that?" I asked.

"Indian."

"Indian?"

"This is a reservation."

"A reservation?"

"Yes."

We went on. And on and on. We got into something that looked unlogged, finally, much thicker, and it filtered out much of the rain, which produced a lightness of sorts in the new denser woods—it felt suddenly rather cheery, like springtime. I thought of Johnny Weissmuller swinging through transplanted monkeys. I thought of white women. I thought of many things inexplicable in their timing when the truly inexplicable arose before me: a castle, or something. My second impression was a hospital, my third was that it was a mansion for the so impossibly rich (a Vanderbilt house, say) that they'd abjured location, location, location. I could not picture the substructure necessary to hold it up in this swamp.

It—the building—looked to be about five hundred feet across its brown stone face and to have been built by Mussolini. This was the kind of thing you'd be taken to in South Carolina and it would have a hallowed, understated name like Brick House and would have been owned by a haunted family like Seabrook, but now Ted Turner would own it and there'd be actresses, Jane or no, naked on the roof beside the (new) pool. But it wouldn't be the size of a hospital. It would be human-scaled, if large—entertainable, that is— and therefore all the more prepossessing. This monstrosity was industrial. It was unlit. I supposed it, somehow, connected to "Indians," whatever that meant.

In anticipating Indians, I was close. The thing was full of what you'd call hippies, for want of a better term. There was every stripe of lost person under fifty, and some older, in the joint, and a couple of Charlie Manson leaders and a couple of Dennis Hopper loons and a couple of Mama Cass sandwich eaters, and in one room I believe I saw a ring of praying pygmies.

"We are looking for game violations and we won't find any," Taurus told me. "I wanted you to see this." We went all through the house, which I'd estimate at a hundred rooms. It was three stories and had big hallways as if it *had* been intended for industrial use of some kind. In the basement there was a swimming pool with water in it the color and consistency of sugarcane juice and two small alligators in that green porridge.

"There's your game violation," I said.

"No, that's not a game violation. They can't keep them out. Let's go smoke a peace pipe."

We went upstairs and met with a redheaded guy who seemed equivalent to a Secretary of State. I had the immediate feeling he represented in his hale, bluff cheer some darker and more ornery political figure—one of the Mansons skittering around, perhaps. This guy was coming on like a Kiwanis man. He got us some beer from a chest freezer in a hall, the only appliance I saw in the place, and I don't know what powered it, if anything—the beer was hot. Women passed us in tie-dyed outfits, looking bucolically purposeful—they'd just meet your eye before looking away, slowly, at the baseboards, as they walked, hips swaying, on. A newsletter of sorts was on the chest freezer, which was serving as a bar. It had a headline that read US: 111, AMERIKA: O.

I couldn't figure who Us was. I listened. Us, it would seem, was every bedraggled fool between California and Italy who'd got a *real* nose for the real thing in counterculture. This was a prototype failed orphanage, sort of, or summer camp, sort of, built by Huey Long for the children of workers and never inaugurated or celebrated or even decorated. And it sat in the vast Atchafalaya Basin without the highway and the bridge that would have connected it to the capitalist world from which it was to have offered socialist children refuge. It was all Rastas and nutria now. It was appalling and delightful.

Suddenly the Secretary of State was putting himself between me and a new arrival, a man yelling at me. Taurus took the moment to get another beer from the chest freezer on which we'd been leaning. The yeller was saying, "That's exactly our problem! That fucker *is* the problem!"

I sized him up. Not too big but crazed, and not crazed enough to be ineffective. The Secretary of State turned him and ushered him out of the room, a big sunroom facing the bayou we'd come in on.

"I apologize. Sometimes . . ."

"I'm sure," I said. And I was. I was sure that this kind of sumping was the left-wing equivalent of a Klan rally or a dogfight. It was a teeming boil of maladjusts who were, failing everything else, going to be *heroes* to the people. They hadn't a goddamned clue as to who "the people" was, beyond their deprived, righteous selves. I was not unsympathetic to them, at least not given the predictable responses of my father and his cronies to a scene like this, but personally and privately and without fanfare I would have enjoyed biting the yeller's nose off. Taurus handed me a beer and steered me out of there and told the Secretary of State he would regard all hogs in the area as feral, huntable.

At first I thought he was referring somehow to their women, that he was mad, too. Then I saw he wasn't.

"These hippies eat meat?" I asked.

"They do."

"They grow rice?"

"They grow pot. Got pot plants in here bigger than Christmas trees."

•

We rode out, suddenly in sun. There were red-eared sliders on logs and bright green astroturfy bogs of duckweed, and sacalait were snapping bugs under the duckweed like .22 shorts. I could have fished. I could have fished and looked each crappie in his red-rimmed eye and been thankful I was, whatever I was, not a hippie in Huey Long's orphanage. I thought of frying up a mess of fish out in this gone place and eating them, and then thought of the Ameses coming over to eat with us. I could do without that. I was not disappointed to see that Taurus was taking me to my car.

We got there and tied up, and it was apparent that, not unlike during his earlier tutelage of me, he had most deliberately and most subtly shown me precisely something he wanted me to see. Was it what lies at the absolute end of the road of dalliance? A Land's End of softheadedness? Was it the monsters of sexuality that await you if you can't recognize a good thing and glom onto it? There were those good women of mine, and at least that good-legged mother o' mine of his . . . I would never figure the fellow out, and that itself was part of the lesson he still provided. There is enigma. There is enigma.

I thanked him and he was on his way. I knew as much as I am to know about my mother's ex-lover game warden bayou stud to nurses and protector of hippies felling pot plants the size of Christmas trees. I could imagine them out there sawing at the trees with butter knives they found in the orphanage. I went to New Orleans.

22 / IN NEW ORLEANS I stayed at the Flamingo Bar & Grill & Hotel—a place I began to gather was famous. It was removed from the Quarter just a bit in space, but in spirit it was miles away: it was the final resting place for boozists, remove all pretense to Catholic this, voodoo that, and Creole this and that. It was three stories that wound away from the street, not one floor level, with a grill & bar in which you could eat and drink twenty-four hours a day. Beside the pay phone a hand-lettered sign read, "Imaginary conversations prohibited." I spent some time in this grill, which was Norman Rockwell meets William Burroughs, if Burroughs was, as we say, the dominant partner in such a twain. It was so creepy it was most agreeable. You mostly wanted to drink your beer, which they did not begrudge you at any hour, without anyone talking to you lest you might have to smell him. I spent time there in lieu of forced march to the known touring nodes, and looked at my gently bubbling yellow beer in a good heavy water glass that had fine scars on it from years of use, and thought of my mother, mostly. It has come to this, I thought. I was

drinking, but not drunk—I was in Hotel Step 13 and looking like a long-term registered guest (one day I got my shoes on the wrong feet and discovered the unlevel floors more manageable that way).

I found in my coat pocket—I have noted that the true secrets of the universe are discovered in sport- and suit-coat pockets either during or after drunkenness—a note from Patricia Hod. We were in the habit of giving each other love letters, I guess you'd call them, little scraps of mostly excess sentiment we'd have been too embarrassed to say aloud, things we could at once safely laugh at and believe. She had given it to me a day or two before the walkout, and I had looked at it, glanced at it, during the emergency soup-tureen foster-homing and rearguard retreat and tangled minutiae of fleeing women you don't want to know you are fleeing—so I had only glanced at it. It was written before she knew there was anything wrong—I thought. But in New Orleans's Hotel Step 13 beneath a sign prohibiting imaginary conversations, with my shoes on the opposite feet, and getting profoundly homesick for something *nice*—I kept thinking about *Southern Living* modern-bathroom ads with toilet bibs matching the bathmats—this note leapt out of my pocket and un-creased itself stiffly and resonated plainly in the hand like a lost biblical tract. "I see," Patricia Hod had written me two days before I unfairly left her (*wanting* her, too), "your mother's face in yours sometimes. Not always. But sometimes. It's disturbing when you see that in a man's face."

That it was. It disturbed me there and then. That she saw that, that she said that, that she had seen it in other men, that it disturbed her in the cases of these other men, that it disturbed her in my case, that my case was not different from that of other men, or was it? (It would be if she saw the face she *should* have seen in mine: *her* mother's, sister to my father.) Was this disturbing mom's face in one's man merely the latest case, or was it disturbing for reasons other, maybe better and real reasons: maybe Patricia Hod loved me. This idea winged too near me like a bat in the dark in the fluorescent glare of the Flamingo Bar & Grill. Maybe she was not crazy—*I* was crazy. This is a notion we all articulate on a daily basis, inspired by a thousand daily things, and I was leery of it, half-drunk on skid row in a town I did not and did not want to understand.

Patricia Hod. Would Patricia Hod have me back? She shouldn't, that we knew. She possibly couldn't—gone, etc. But she was crazy! There was hope. I got a beer and eyed the pay phone and deigned not: the prospect of such a call— and to where? Her mother's house, where her mother drank so much her father shipped her out to sleep with her cousin? To my own house, where I'd left her and where my own mother drank so much she put her up, *for me?*—the prospect of such a call was too imaginary. Under the circumstances I thought the sign prohibiting imaginary conversations had been conceived just for me. Beer. Beer was going to have to go, and I was going to have to put my shoes on the right feet, shortly. I got another beer and stretched out my splayed feet and thought about that. Norman Rockwell was going to get up and say, Mr. Burroughs, I'm not taking it anymore. I find finally untenable your acquiescence to the *disgusting* in human endeavor. Put your pants on, Mr. Burroughs, I am through with you. This was amusing, and a bit sad, but I'd reached the point where I had to concede Mr. Rockwell right.

So I resolved to go home, passing the Jax Beer Brewery and discovering it converted to the Jackson Brewery Mall and selling, among other things, fiberglass pirogues and faux Izod shirts with the alligator replaced by tiny crayfish, and to collect my cousin Patricia.

·

Oh, Patricia Hod. You are thirty and firm and dazed of head, but you are all of that. You lay with me for a month under the scrutiny of my mother and did not run or whimper or rail or fret. You lay there *like a man*. I ran like a boy, but we are going to overlook all of that. That is to be overlooked. Overlook that. Overlook me. Look me over. Look at me, Patricia Hod. I come to you ruined and smiling and smart. You can do much much much worse than this, Patricia Hod. I can put my chinos on one leg at a time, like everybody else (though I cannot work for certain boys in Atlanta wearing them like everybody else), or I can jump into them like a fireman, or I can jump out of my chinos like a man on fire. I and my chinos are changeable, Patricia Hod.

Outside the Flamingo Bar & Grill it began to rain. The marquee was lit by ordinary incandescent lightbulbs, which stuck nakedly out of individual porcelain sockets. I wondered how many of them lit when the switch was thrown. It was a simple matter to replace the blown bulbs. A stepladder, some bulbs, a gentleman sober enough to stand and deliver. The world was mine. The world is anybody's if you will square off and hit it.

This is something I have learned, and I think I have learned it in time. I have learned it, I think, and continue to learn it, I think, from women.

23 / I THOUGHT OF the ways you approach the abandoned. It is not unlike the rabid: will they hide from you or charge? I thought the least advisable strategy would be weeping for forgiveness. At the other end of the spectrum of the untenable would be promising the abandoned forgiveness. Somewhere in the resonant middle ground was a posture of defiant culpability that offered restitution of the way it was before. I was not looking forward to this articulation before a woman who had drowned cats and set fires before subsiding into lost-love catatonia in London. On the other hand, and this was partly why Patricia Hod was looming so attractive, you could not imagine approaching an ingenue under these terms. She'd see the matter too clearly: *you left*. The End. You wanted a woman who saw your leaving as a matter of necessary and sophisticated contradiction: rose mole stipple upon a trout; oh, brindled cow. Oh, fall down. Then get up. You *needed* a Calamity Jane for these affairs, or Annie Oakley. Dale Evans was out. Dale would wait for Roy, and Roy, bless his heart, would never

be short, late, wrong, impotent, drunk, or out of key. I will woo but I will not croon.

I seized the pay phone and called Patricia Hod's house in Columbia. Her mother, my aunt who goes on such vicious toots that the attending alcoholics seek medical counsel for her, answered. "Well, well, Marster Simons." This is an upcountry slur of the low country. "How *do* you do?"

"I do fine, Aunt Sasa. Is Patricia there?"

"I *thought* that might be what you'd ask. Have you ever seen Pat Boone? I can't *stand* him."

I heard a loud, shouted voice in the background: "DON'T SAY THAT! YOU JUST DON'T KNOW HIM WELL ENOUGH!"

My aunt, apparently responding to this, said, "What?"

And the voice said, somewhat less loud: "You just don't *know* him well enough."

"Who?" my aunt asked.

"Whoever you said you can't stand," the voice said.

"I *said*," my aunt said, "I can't stand *Pat Boone*."

"Oh," said the voice, which I'd now identified as my uncle's. "I thought you meant someone you knew."

"Jesus Christ Almighty," my aunt said, returning her attention to the phone. "Patricia's not here. *She's on a date*." My aunt zinged this in like an Amazon sharpshooter. It was her way of saying she had the whole story, the whole score, and had taken a position in it, apparently, not surprisingly on Patricia's side. But this was complex: Patricia and I together was likely to be something she would, against the rest of the family excepting *my* mother, side with, so she would probably not render Patricia altogether unavailable to me. She would just tender some difficulty. "She's out with a fellow named Johnny Ham," she said, and I heard her take a drink. Then she whispered, "I can't stand him."

I started laughing and she did, too.

"Aunt Sasa," I said. "Tell you what. Would you, ah, tell Patricia to meet me in Edisto?"

"In *Edisto*," she said, with several kinds of false shock in her tone. What for? After you *left* her there? Why *should* she? Etc. I could only assume she knew the circumstances, but it was the kind of thing, also, where she might just be gratuitously saying "In *Ed*isto?" In *Af*rica? In *Ohio*? In the *yard*? Out*side*?

"At the house," I said. "There is a key in the A/C compressor. I will be there in three days."

My aunt said then, gravely, "I have never gotten *a thing* I wanted from this family."

"I can't stand it, either, Aunt Sasa."

"I hope," she said, taking another ice-clunking gulp of something, "you get what you want. Bye."

I held that ambiguous phone in the air in the Flamingo Bar & Grill for a moment, wondering if it meant she'd tell Patricia or would not tell Patricia, and put it down finally, worried suddenly about the imaginary-conversation prohibition. I'd had a most real conversation, but no one would believe it.

24 / JAKE'S LOOKED CLOSED, so I did
not stop. It would have been nice to lay in a trunkful of
provisions against Patricia's absence or presence—this was
going to be a trek either way. The joint (Jake's) looked
abandoned in the way that only the truly bereft business
can: the only difference between its countenance when
closed and when doing business hand over fist is a padlock
on the door. With his bank-vault door he didn't need a padlock. Somewhere behind it Jake lived, either in the room
behind and above the bar or in the house out back where
his mother had lived. It was a shack covered in rolled linoleum brick siding, or possibly the stuff was composition
asphalt; it had never occurred to me to feel it once I understood it wasn't brick. Was there, or should there be, anything
particularly telling about a people who would have wood
houses look like brick and Cadillacs that look like giant June
bugs? I trusted, prowling by Jake's and easing into our road,
that I weren't going into racial mope. I had done enough
of that as a child.

I had other fish to fry. At best I had a house with a

madwoman with Thoroughbred legs who could swim the English Channel in it whom I thought I wanted. In this time I had formed a specific portrait of Patricia Hod, for which I longed: a quiet woman with troubles aplenty at home and abroad that you found in your bed accepting not simply you but your mother's steerage of you into that bed (and your mother's face in yours) and the new set of problems you brought with you. A woman who took it as it came, with (I had come to appreciate) no lip-biting apprehensiveness. She breathed, as it were, through her mouth. What *was* Patricia Hod? Patricia Hod was a girl from God. That's what, or who, Patricia Hod was. It is true that I felt a little bogused by my recent endeavors, in which there had been enough booze alone to account for my feeling like a fish on its side, flaring its gills and with its one fixed eye looking at the world and its grim chances. Suffice it to say I entered the tunnel of palmetto leading to my mother's quaint and now vintage, once splendid and now modest beach house feeling perhaps not dissimilar to that fish. I was also feeling poetic. It felt—things—as if it was about to rain. It was a Monday, as near as I could make out, a rural Monday of the sort that you could tell it wasn't Sunday by the absence of church traffic but you could not be sure if it was Monday because of the absence of work traffic. It was a stillborn Monday giving you the post-church, agreeable creeps. All I could ever think of on these kinds of mornings was that if I had to make a living, which inexplicably presented at these moments the idea of driving to a factory-line position in Pittsburgh, I'd *know* it was Monday morning, and it was infinitely better to be simply driving by neutron-bombed Jake's Baby Grand and the whole gassed low country and

guessing it was Monday. The palmettos had a stilled, expectant edge to them, too, and the house sat plainly where
it was supposed to. No car.

That I took to be that. It was a disappointment surprising
in its force. Why Patricia Hod meant this much to me I
could not have said. The *deliberate* not saying before, during
our little month's halcyon, accounted, though, for part of
the force now that the cat, as it were, was out of the bag.
I was holding a bag of sorts. It was empty. The house looked
stolid, the beach brave, the surf as fine and brutal, as gentle
and seductive, as . . . as it always does. I couldn't stand this
aloneness. I could not recall suffering it like this before. It
brought the Southern Historian to mind: Maybe he was
inexplicably, irrepressibly lonely, too, and that is why if you
put cameras on him in his study and told him to tell apocrypha about, say, Custer, he wept. "The Wawer! The
Wawer!" really meant "I'm lonely! Don't you . . . *Yankees*
ever get *lonely*? No, of course you don't. Y'all have
never . . . *lost!*"

•

I went back up to Jake's and marched around back to the
old house where I didn't know for sure he was staying but
which I wanted to see. It had none of the fake-brick siding
I'd remembered but looked vaguely creosoted and vaguely
painted brightly about the windows—some Mediterranean
blue had chipped down to some white, or off-white, giving the
window trim the look of china. Beside the house, where the
dog that I diagnosed as having mice in his ears (a remark
that charmed two generations of militant slave descendants
into liking this unmilitant slave-owner descendant) had

been chained, was that dog's rear axle, driven into the ground, and on the axle the chain the dog had worn in its constant prowl and yelp and circling for release until it had been released, forever. *That bulldog got its Patricia Hod*, I thought, standing there beside Jake's shack, and took a leak. *Don't forget, you're an architect* came the next thought, so improbably that I looked over my head to see if there were an absurd balloon above it. What I saw was Jake's face studying me from a window of the house.

"What the fuck?" he said.

"Jake!"

"Peein' on the house!"

"No. Just here, Jake." I took a step away so he could see my lack of harm. I should have told him an architect would never pee on a house.

"Allreetden," Jake said.

As protocol suggested, I waited for Jake to come out. I looked in the dog's excavated hole—it looked like an old Confederate earthwork, come to think about it—to make sure nothing of mine had run in it, which at that moment seemed a worse profanation than peeing on the house. It hadn't. The urine would have stood in that dry bowl like spit on face powder. I remembered clearly at that moment my having as a child spit on the Doctor's face powder. It would roll harmlessly around and you could pour it off. Perhaps I was mistaking it for shoe polish, her powder, in tins and cakes like the old man's pucks of Kiwi wax that you were *supposed* to spit on—

"What you *doin'* heah?"

"Supposed be a woman at my house and they ain't."

He took a long look at me and then beyond me toward

the Grand, as if looking for others, whether for help or for a compounding of this trouble I couldn't say.

"So what," he said, very distinctly, "is the prob-lem?"

"I don't know."

"Spose be a woman at *all* our house and ain't."

"I *know* that," I said, and it almost made us both laugh.

"So why you up here peein' *on my house* what I want to know."

"Where's that worm pit you had around here?"

"That what?"

"Worm pit."

"*Woim* pit?"

"Yeah."

"What in hell a *woim* pit?"

"Pit with worms in it."

"*Pit*?"

"Yeah."

"Ain't no *pit*. They *woim* round heah, ain' need no *pit*."

"You had a pit, a good pit."

"You are peein' on man's house before business hour say he got woims in a *pit*. I had a *pit* I know I have a *pit*."

"What happened to this dog?" I indicated the earthworks.

"What dog?"

I picked up and hefted the chain, a good heavy one. "This dog."

"That a *chain*."

At this point he was self-consciously scudging me, as Athenia was wont to put it. We'd lost the fine moment of genuine humor we'd had—a miracle that we'd had such a moment, really. I felt like going fishing—the same kind of emotion I'd had in Louisiana when being shown the door by Taurus. Here I was, being shown the door in Edisto. After a certain point, in life or in the modern world, I'm not sure, you can't go fishing when being shown the door. You can't go fishing again.

"Jake, do I owe you for any beer or anything?"

"I don't know."

"Well, can you give me that soup tureen I left here?"

"That casserole thing?"

"Yeah."

He went back in the house and came out wearing, I swear to God, a pair of high heels and carrying a large dildo of the sort—squeeze bulb and all—I had seen on the roadside months ago in Texas.

"What's that?" I said.

"This? Oh. This something somebody *left* heah."

"I see. And those?" I indicated, falling in alongside him, the shoes.

"These something somebody left heah, too."

That covered it. Inside the Grand, Jake rang up a case of beer and I paid him—I did not want it, but it seemed the neighborly thing to do under the circumstances. He found the tureen, which had an errant cue ball in it. He put the dildo and the shoes in a paper grocery sack and wrote *You* on it and put the bag behind the bar. His own boots were sitting neatly on the bar itself.

"Thanks, Jake."

"Anytime."

I left. I felt much, much better. It was still gloomy, purple, with a promise of a light but steady rain, but there was a little wind, as if what was in the offing was something better. It was July. It was early for hurricane, but possible. My hurricane kit does not include window tape and batteries and bottled water and radios. I buy ice and liquor, do *all* the laundry, vacuum the house. I watch the television until the comic, brave reporters doing everything they are insisting we not do—these are invariably women reporters, I've noticed—are blown in their sexy yellow sou'westers from the frame. When that goes off, watch the ocean and pray for direct hit. I went home.

25 / BEFORE I HEARD or saw anything I felt a humidity that was unusual in a closed house and then immediately smelled a smell that was entirely strange in a closed *or* open house, and it was a wet sweetness that announced, a second before she appeared herself, in a terry-cloth robe cinched tight, with her bare feet and bare chest matching in their dark, moist, firm contrast to the terry cloth—and over that a towel turbaned on her head making her look like Queen Nefertiti, the same rig my mother wore—Patricia Hod.

She stood there with her lips pursed in mid-gesture, waiting for me to decide things. I stood there too long, so she went on to her (my) room as she had been going.

I followed her into the room, where she was at work in the mirror doing something to her eyebrows. I still couldn't come up with anything to say. I managed to remember that she had somehow appeared here the first time as well without benefit of telltale car.

"What did *that* prove, and what does *this* prove?" Patricia Hod said.

I wrestled this one right to the floor and held it there best I could: "I was nervous and now I'm not. Or now I'm—"

"Now you're lonely. Now you're brave. *Now* you're a man. Now you're a *true* coward. You blew it. Do I have it right?" And she turned back to the mirror in her tall white Nefertiti headdress and readdressed her eyebrows, arching them and licking a pencil and holding it braced against her forehead with a little finger out in space like an outrigger for balance, the way a Southern pulp heroine would drink a Coke from one of the little bottles you can't get anymore, at least not the returnable kind with the proper mix in it. You could in the days when they had cocaine in them and you had people, innocent, solid people like this girl and not unlike me, for example, addicted to them, especially in the morning, in lieu of coffee—people who would graduate at some point in the day to liquor and reinvoke, or reinvent, the South. What was left of the South, its reinvention or its convention, was in her errant, gorgeous, hi-ho little finger, which stood out like a vestigial antenna in the perfumy air of her. This still air was separated from the air of the Atlantic Ocean by an Andersen window and Corning fiberglass and Georgia-Pacific T-1-11 siding and Wal-Mart house paint. On this side of all that, her finger was poised in the charged humid air of a showered fresh woman who wasn't—it just barely was occurring to me—freshly showered for nothing. "What are you standing there like that for? Don't fripper it up," she said, turning and coming to me, a little less brave-looking herself.

In standing my ground I signed a little contract with fine clauses I did not want to read then or ever. I kissed Patricia Hod, and she was kissing me, with *ink*.

I did not fripper it up.

There is central air conditioning and there is another air, not central, not conditioned. I was resting easy in it, deigning not fripper.

26 / AND WHAT OF MY MOTHER? What of the Doctor who bade me become seer and sayer and has had to content herself so far with a visionless architect shacked up with his cousin? She does not disapprove. She does not despair. Potato salad comes to mind.

My mother, the Doctor, is capable of a kind of iconic metonymy that will steer her, and you, if you allow it, through the complex dance of despairing, fretting, bourgeois others about you. If you can have metonymy when those about you are losing theirs, she implies, you'll be a man. She does this not infrequently with food. In a case I am thinking of recently, it was potato salad.

There was a family reunion of sorts scheduled—unique in this our fractured dissolute clan. There has not been an earnest reunion under that name that purported to include all living members of this kennel since a time I vaguely recall that included, among other things, some beer bottles left in a freezer too long, resulting in frozen ropes of beer and glass that resembled small intestines, with children playing with the intestines and adults cussing and others laughing and those cussing going to Jake's and those laughing continuing to laugh and the children getting cut as they were warned not to. That was a long time ago. There was a snake shot on the beach during that convocation, as I recall. Snakes now know the health hazards of appearing on the open beach. There has most certainly not been a reunion that included our upland lessers—Winn and Sasa and Patricia Hod, among others—since then.

But lo! Patricia Hod was already, like the Yankees torturing our boys during the Wawer, down heah, so someone called the question. A reunion. An unheard-of reunion that just happened to tacitly acknowledge that the uplander clan we should include was already present in a vigorous and apparently lasting knot of first-rate consenting incest. "Potato salad," my mother gets on the phone from Hilton Head to say. "You do that. I'll do that. And Sasa will do that. Then, well, we have it."

"We have what, Mother?"

"A reunion, with enough potato salad."

"I see."

"I have never, Son, had the courage to do what I *really* wanted to do." She let this ride out there for a while. I refused to question her meaning. I knew the meaning. As her man Taurus would show you the nadir of sexual opportunity on a lost bayou and an institutional assortment of *ur* hippies to scare you back into the batter's box, my mother would show the hapless relations potato salad on the hands of the incestuous. The Dinah Shore covered dish on the Sade plates. "Have Patricia make a hot German style if she will, or you make it, and I'll do, you know, my *Joy of Cooking* mayo with potato in it, and Sasa can do that, too, or . . ."

I waited. She never completed the sentence.

"Bye." She was gone. It was the same *bye* Sasa had used: curt, frisky, looking-forward-to-something farewells coming from these profoundly disappointed women happily marrying children to cousins.

•

Potato salad in the South is nothing less than the principal smuggler of cholesterol into the festive, careless heart. It is pure poison beneath the facade of bland puritan propriety. It is the food of choice at any fond banquet of smiling relatives who celebrate tacitly among themselves the dark twining of two of their promising youth. My mother thinks this way instinctively. She can provide the deconstructive grid, but she prefers just *doing* it. And I must say she is good at it.

At the reunion there were the three bowls of potato salad, and they were provided by the mother of the son in the incest tango, the mother of the daughter in the incest tango, and the son and the daughter in the incest tango. The four of us ate the three potato salads Communion-style until we were Confirmed to the gills.

My mother and my aunt Sasa demonstrate a curious non-speaking solidarity in all of this, and I've come to think of them as rival tribal chiefs with iron livers. They approve, each, of her child and the other's child, but they don't deign chat. A kind of silent crossing of arms, liver to liver, as it were.

Sasa tries a bite of the Doctor's potato salad, says, nodding,

"Manny"—the rare affectionate diminutive for her customary "Dr. Manigault," slur of low-country eggheads—and the Doctor tries a bite of Sasa's potato salad, says, nodding, "Sasa." Patricia Hod and I cavort in the lee of this détente of mothers. Neither of them will have another bite of food all day and neither of them has cooked a meal in twenty years.

27 / THE FATHERS ARE FEEBLE. That, I am beginning to deduce, is the father's lot in life. He enfeebles himself when he releases upstream the several million protozoans that engender a tender creature not unlike him but *not enough unlike him,* swimming downstream toward him—they have yellow footprints for the father painted on delivery-room floors, I hear—and toward his radically inexpert but presumptuous guidance. This is enfeebling. This *defines* feeble. So my old man and Patricia Hod's old man, the kind of guys who had Parker shotguns and shot birds when there were birds, who know the whole skinny of the secular, who call a spade a spade or, failing that, have another drink and look at the interest points— these guys just stand there. Looks like a good piece of ass, my old man must think. *Damned* good, Patricia Hod's old man counters. And that is that: feeble progenitors with the dog of incest at their Rotarian heels. I never have had direct contact with either of them on this.

My father's prostate vigilance has been successful: the gland has enlarged to the size of a "baking spud," as it is hilariously put at the Yacht Club of a Saturday afternoon. (Early in that afternoon, too—these fellows do not waste the day like their landlubber inferiors doing eighteen; they walk down to see what's been stolen off the boat and go get a drink and play cards, eighteen or so holes of that.) All the finger probing by his childhood friend and protector has netted him the security of *knowing* there is an expanding baking potato inside him. This is one of many reasons why a man might keep his counsel when his son takes up an attractive taboo, I suppose.

Another might be that I do indeed manage a species of Republican portfolio. I build a handsome building ten or twelve times a year and reduce the coast another ten- or twelve-thousandth in its handsomeness. *They ain't making any more of it* is what you chant when you haul onto site (palmettoed dune) your transit and plumb bob. I have annuity. It will not mature for thirty years, but I myself appear to be coming in under the wire. At this the Republican father can cross his arms and smile in the fat-cat sunshine. That the son may be Sade only makes the cat grin. These are the morals of the proper. The proper truss themselves so well that their herniations prove relief. Even thinking about my old man makes me talk like an idiot. Withal, I dislike him not. For the father provides beyond a definition of the feeble a benchmark of error: sons are given to make one fewer error in life than that which sired them. *One.* To youth this task appears laughably easy. Then . . . well, you begin to see that the scale and scope and kind of error available is proliferating like everything else. Error is on a microchip today. In 1940 it was on an adding machine you had to have two hands and a strong arm to operate. I think this. I apply for help—but counseling, another aspect of the proliferation of error in our time, is quicksand in these my littoral terms.

In the progenitor's view, I've set out on a broken-field run as imprudent as they get but redeemed by the nature of the ball I carry: to his mind, the ball of carnal desire. I have noticed less protest in life from those you expect it from if the case is made or can be made that those getting away with something *are* getting away with something. The petty thief is to be shot, but the larcenist—who *wanted* it, and by God *got* it—is a hero. If I'd showed up, say, as a teenager, with my blue steel and a black girl, it could not have been tolerated past a weekend. But show up closer to thirty years old with your cousin beaming on your arm, your cousin looking truly marvelous, and you feeling truly marvelous, and there is a line of men forming to tell you, sometimes literally, *Go for it!*

At his club we have a weekly set-to which I do not regularly enough avoid, and at one of these—shortly after it became known that the Hod affair, tawdry enough in its first phase, with matronly low-country chaperone present and upcountry approval, was back on, and now without chaperone and approbation—the Progenitor said, apropos of nothing, I thought, just stirring his drink with a red swizzle which he would shortly remove and place neatly on his napkin, diagonally from corner to corner, a red-and-white Diver Down flag, "Everybody has their shit."

"What?"

"Everybody has their shit."

I laughed. "I suppose they do."

He looked at me. "You *know* they do." This is his use of the imperative. He is not saying that I know by experience of what he speaks, but that I had best *believe* what he says. It is economical and annoying in the extreme.

It was only then that I got in the ballpark, or, more precisely, realized I'd been standing at the plate taking this brushback pitch. I got ready, now that I knew the count (0–2), for another pitch. Here it came.

"And everybody's shit *stinks*."

Ah yes. The sentiments of the civilized man. The man that Leakey found and Darwin propounded along his trail of betterment and NASA aided to take giant steps for mankind on the moon. I drank my drink. It was like being a teenager again: Let them have their godawful say and get out of their way. This had been called by my father in its day my "being Cochise." Now, again, I sat there being Cochise. I was Cochise with a martini. I was Cochise with a red plastic sword through his olive, talking to the Great White Father, who was giving Cochise sage and worldly exempli that perhaps his own native gods would not know about. Cochise was probably only getting things like "All things are one" from his own godhead, so he needed "Everybody has their shit" from the Great White Father.

Life is not prevailing. Life is letting those who insist on it prevail around you and preserving a measure of dignity for yourself on the fringe of the embarrassment. The meek *shall* inherit the earth if they can wait out the prodigious period of presumption.

28 / MY PROWESS AS a coastal architect rests on certain indissoluble premises. These include but are not limited to the following: find a way to put the woman into a house that suggests to her she is the widow of a sailor (a cupola with widow's walk may be too overt for a Southern woman, but not for one from Ohio—she will be pleasantly haunted by it); put the man into a house that suggests his main job in life is to be a good host and a good host's main job is to see that everyone has a drink (for the Southern man, a big bar on the main floor reminiscent of a fraternity house; for the man from Ohio, a small bar on every floor, including the basement, for which a facsimile must be made by closing in the support pillars); convince both the man and the woman that the elevations of the house are intimately and uniquely in communion with the elevations of the lot on which it is to sit. This last is most easily accomplished by having no relationship whatsoever between elevations. If this is noticed, speak of "tension" and sweep your arm toward the roiling Atlantic.

Any difficulties to this point can be resolved by attention

to surface. Nothing so puts to rout a couple worrying about whether they are or are not to have, finally, their dream home as some somber revelations about *surface*—its texture, its color, its "integrity." In the toughest of cases, those not stampeded by integrity of surface, I have used "degree of dimensional and cultural stability." There is not a home buyer in this country in my experience who will fight with that. What is culturally stable of course is the pastel. They have seen the corresponding "earth tones" on the black shacks and jooks, and the garish neons on the roadhouses and motels that surround but do not include the pristine marsh they are colonizing, and none of that bold poor downtrod color will leak out here into the clean, salty, expensive air. Yet there are some sophisticates who resent what they recognize as the undemocratic pastel, typically objecting to "blandness." For these hearty pioneers you must be ready with alternative pasteling. This is a snap, because alternative pasteling is historical, and if there is any stronger, finer irony than selling a brand-new house by claiming it historical, I do not know what it is. I stain the outside—before there was paint, all wood was treated with stains, usually involving blood ("rubricated with animal products")—and I pickle the inside. Pickling is in fact my middle name. You can take a job away from an architect talking about faux marbling with paint and sponges if you walk up and pickle a piece of trim before their very eyes. Because it precedes paint (modern paint is corporate swagger, fruit of research & development, therefore undemocratic) and because it looks innocuous and yet is authentic, pickling will convince the most hard-to-sell egalitarian dream-home builder.

I have good relations with framing carpenters. These are

fellows holding useless advanced degrees and very useful 28-ounce Estwing rip hammers. They wear short pants and blond boots that they refuse to oil, and are sun-blond themselves and smoke pot well and frame well. They are what is left of the political ambition of the just post-Vietnam American hippie, if there is such a thing—political ambition in a hippie (and there is, if Dr. Bronner's peppermint soap is soap). I like to show up about quitting time with a case of beer, when only the framers are still at a job, and sit in the open, upper rooms with them to ostensibly look over the plans, which I roll out on the plywood subfloor and pin down with beers and invite them to comment on—whether the headers are over- or underbuilt or how they feel about all these skylights. The post-'Nam hippie framer falls into two camps on skylights: those who did not go favor skylights, the more the better; those who went condemn them as dreamy invitations to perpetual roof leaks—if you want light, put in windows, real ones, and beyond that buy some light fixtures and pay to run them. You do not cheat the light of day by cutting holes in the roof. A framer who went will let a framer who did not go do all the skylights on a job.

"Do you think this house messes up the beach too much?"

"What?" the framer who went will say. "Mess up *the beach*?"

"You've been as considerate as you could be, I think," the framer who did not go will interrupt, prompting a long look from the framer who went.

That's about as far as you want to go into the issue of beach hugging with framers whose livelihood depends on beach mauling, whether they went or didn't. But this is a nice moment in your dubious occupation, drinking beer and smelling the faint ammonia of the plans and the good salt air and the perennial whiff of pot on these guys who do the actual, honest, hands-on beach mauling, driving their twelvepenny nails into your white, white spruce all the live-long day, sitting with you a moment in your respective philosophical reposes. You are not such a bad guy for a suit, and they of course are not such bad guys for grunts. A sunset under these conditions, glassy waves catching the last pink light, a green marsh catching a sudden chill and stopping even its fiddler ticking, and turning gray, can be a most agreeable thing.

29 / WE HAVE BEEN KNOWN to spend an evening up at Jake's. The first of these was memorable, because no one else was there and Jake was free to romp with us in racial set pieces, and because I learned that my friend Jinx had died. Patricia and I went in, feeling smart and secure in each other, as we are wont to do, to have a drink and to establish her as a credit customer there should we ever need it. The place was bone empty, 9:30 on a Monday night.

"Damn, Jake. Where is everybody?"

"Everybody here."

"Where's . . . where's Jinx?" I hadn't seen Jinx, or thought of him, in years.

"Who?"

"Jinx."

"*Know* no Jinx."

"You know, skinny guy. Quiet dude. Played—"

"He dead."

"Dead?" I looked at Patricia—she was looking at me with a kind of told-you-so raised eyebrow, her purse still on her shoulder. I took it and gave it to Jake, and he buried it somewhere behind the bar as if he had hundreds of purses to keep track of. It was funny. He took about three minutes, bent over and unseen behind the bar. Then he popped up, freshened by duty, and said, "Sickle cell."

"Sickle cell what?"

"Sickle cell Jinx. He gone."

"No."

"In the hole."

"How old was he?"

"How I know how *old* is he?"

"Give us the baddest malt liquor there is, Jake. Treat us like brothers."

Jake regarded Patricia. "He like this when he little, too. You in trouble."

"I know it," Patricia said.

Jake was complying. He gave us two tall, totally undrinkable things in gold cans with pictures of cobras on them, and we drank them. The place empty like that—a long flatback hall with the feel of fine glass underfoot on the concrete floor—was austere, stark, frightening. I could recall this friend of mine Jinx playing pinball by himself, drinking alone, smiling at anyone who interrupted him. I recalled, too, how *neat* he was. He had a kind of preppie air to him: pressed, or permanently pressed, polyester shirts and slacks, and dress shoes, the effect of it skewed when you noticed he wore no socks. I remember that. His ankles were nearly the same color as the black shoes into which they fit, and they looked hard and worn and slick as the shoe leather itself. It was like a hoof and a shoe; there was no place for a soft sock in this arrangement. I looked closely at these feet one night, sitting on a stool under the pinball machine. In the days of my childhood celebrity at the Grand, sitting under the pinball machine would prevent people from asking ad nauseam if I had mice in *my* ears. I now noticed the pinball machine was gone.

Jinx was gone, his flashy distraction was gone, I was going somewhere myself. Patricia and Jake were talking, which was what I'd brought her for—if Jake could talk to you, he could give you credit. She could handle herself. I thought of her as an attractive Margaret Thatcher, perverse as that may be. Jinx dead. Of a specifically black menace. There was a day in which I would have been inclined to see that as somehow my fault. I am less inclined to see it that way today. Something I couldn't (or wouldn't) prevent got Jinx, and something he couldn't (or wouldn't) prevent would get me. I had been a pure accommodation of race and racial difference when I sat under a pinball machine and watched Jinx's unsocked feet in their plainness. Now it was as if I were a (self-appointed) representative of the very lowest arm of the State Department trying to head off the very largest war it would ever have, and the last one it wanted to have. I was a chump. Jake knew that and put up with me anyway. I was a paying customer.

Patricia Hod went to the bathroom and Jake interrupted me in these my stately ruminations by settling a new can of Cobra at my place. He shook his head and gave a long whistle in the direction Patricia Hod had gone.

"Shoe fly," he said.

"Amen," I said. I had no idea what "shoe fly" meant. It seemed to be plenty positive.

"The new Duchess," he said.

"Yes, ma'am," I said. I recalled the high-heeled shoes and dildo and wondered if I ought be saying something like that, so I said it again. "Yes, ma'am, Jake. I am in some cotton now."

"You *in* some cotton."

"I am in cotton like . . . like a pistol in a Crown Royal bag." This was how Jake kept—and operated—his bar pistol.

"You got cheetah on your side," he said.

"What?"

"Say you got *cheetah*, man."

"Okay." I had no idea what this meant, either, and Jake knew that, but that was partly his point. It was a compliment that was better for my not entirely getting it. In my current intellectualizing mode, I was ironically *less* a chump if I let it go and did not dig for it, white topical anthropologist. I tried one out myself: "All the snow in the world won't change the color of the pine needles."

"Heard that."

Cheetah came back from the bathroom and we had no more time for our racial minuet. Patricia Hod looked better to me than any single person or thing or idea or place or car or horse or church or God or sandbox or sentry or sentiment or—I kissed her full on the mouth right there, and she *liked* it, looking even as she had to at Jake to apologize, and Jake walked, chuckling, lightly, away.

30 / PATRICIA HOD AND I are dancing on
the beach. It has rained and there is a steady, firm inshore
wind, about twenty knots, and with it regular waves march-
ing in like redcoats. It looks very much like a hurricane,
but I have not bothered to check a radio or anything else.
Should there be one, and bad, Jake's is far enough inland
to not drown and there is always a serious hurricane party
there and I can use it to introduce Patricia to the island.
Patricia Hod is, as Jake notes, heiress to the Duchess, my
mother. I will withhold that she is my cousin. It is the kind
of thing I expect will be known, somehow, and tolerated,
in fact will have a happy life on the drums. This culture
here—it is being called "the culture of indigenous peoples"
by the preservationists who have arrived more often than
not from Washington, D.C. (inexplicably, because they are
not with the government, in fact oppose government), to
help preserve it—this culture, whatever it is, is a very patient, modest, let-others-alone thing that changes, I think,
from day to day in its levels of violence, but beyond that is
steady. It steadily *gets tired* is the other thing I've noticed.

The indigenous are tired, the non-indigenous not. The white, here before the tired black but seen as non-indigenous because they would develop what has not been developed before, are not tired. In fiduciary straits since Sherman scared the pee wine out of them, they now have the condo dollar to revive, in a manner of speaking, the rice and indigo and cotton dollar and raise their heads above the erstwhile worthless ancestral marsh.

Patricia and I go to all manner of *Southern Living* tableaux—to jobs (I make the post-and-beam; Patricia can *sell* them); to families (we are a bedrock of dire breath-holding for the normal folk in our clan: some look to see that she is not pregnant, some to confirm, I-told-you-so, the slouching toward them of our purblind issue); and to the ordinary nexuses on this our bourgeois earth, offices and lobbies and malls. We inhabit the marauding, vigorous, non-indigenous mainland world by day.

By island night it is another matter. I am feeling very good, dancing with my illicit bride (for which I understand African shades would hound us to the grave and beyond). Patricia Hod and I do well in our tribal tabooey, and my mother I think of as the shaman who cast the spell that guarantees the tabooey will go unremarked and unmolested. I worry about my mother's health—the *absence* of baking potato portends worse—but that is what you do with parents after they've quit worrying about yours. Life seems impractically practical in the calm, medium view.

I am dancing with firm, cool Patricia Hod on the firm, cool beach. The sand is packed hard as an infield and breaks when you turn a foot in it with a clean squeak. A damp low wedge of sand marks the turn. The wind is full of salt.

There is the delicious contrast between Patricia Hod's cotton blouse and her smooth, swelling chest, and soon we've marked up the entire beach with this our clumsy waltz, to no music but our own. We will go inside and shower in the slightly rusty water, redolent of iron and sulfur, and emerge smelling as good as a boiled egg (Patricia Hod does to me), and fall on each other like . . . breakfast. I bloom into some kind of monster of happiness in her arms, in her neck, not knowing my name. Beached up on Patricia Hod like this these days, if I were asked for ID I could only pat my pockets, shrug, and go to sleep.

Then start awake—hounded by the old fear: the big picture. I have no idea what the big picture is. Life is a giant proposition put you in terms so elusive and slick and fast that you can but stand before the barker and chuckle, Here's my dollar, I'll play, I must, and I will lose. Some days, some nights, you childishly want to see the rigging, the magnets or the strings, behind the board, under the table, on the wheel. Life is missing things, not getting them.

But I hold Patricia Hod. Her neck is a quarter inch from my nose, which seems to be the instrument with which I record all this wisdom and distribute it to my brain. Her neck is a hollow of tasty hope.

Patricia Hod has a way of stepping out of her bath and confronting you, in her white robe, smelling of soap, with her arms at her sides and standing there as if to say, What are you going to do about *this*? She'll stand there until you do something about it, which for me is to put my mouth into a little spot above her collarbone like a bee going in for pollen. Contact is enough; I don't need to *do* anything, and Patricia doesn't seem to want anything done, particularly.

We stand there in this attitude of carnal handshake. This moment does not want lips, which by contrast are messy and have their agenda and force you both into business that gets complicated, and it does not want breast, which gets things accelerated and infantile and motherly and hysterical. This moment wants a quiet hollow in dark, taut flesh, just my lips, closed, on it, breathing deeply, and looking over her shoulder if the robe falls off I can see down the valley of her back to the rising mountain of serious flesh down there, and things will be serious soon enough. But for the moment, no. Just this succor in this shoulder. Just this kiss, this meat, this pulse beside bone, this cool lonely wind, this me and this you. I am not supposed to even *taste*.

·

And it comes, does it, to this? To hiding with the (wrong) little woman? Hiding from what? From "greatness"? From *saying* something? The things my mother had in mind for me? Do not all our mothers have them in mind for all of us?

In Patricia Hod I am hiding, then. I am seeking refuge, moreover, from no persecution. That was the bane, the only irritant in the pleasant oyster of my days. From nothing I flee, into *less* nothing. *You* save us, and let your mother know you've done it. I have saved myself, and I have saved myself the saving.

"Jake," I'm going to say some night shortly, "save us. I'm not going to save us."

"Who?"

"Any of us."

"We save," he'll say.

"Hilton Head's coming, man. Buy you out. Cut your trees. That cash register be a computer. Washington, D.C., coming, man. People be in here knock *you* in the head."

"Got that now." He produces the Crown Royal bag. He smiles broadly.

"The Wawer!" I say. "The Wawer!"

Jake looks at his pistol in its purple velvet bag. He does not investigate, at all, this thing I'm saying. What can he think I'm saying?

I am saying that either I gave up before the battle began or there was no war to fight, I cannot tell. If there was a war—even if it is but the war of human potential, which today looks, militarily speaking, less winnable than ever before—and one chooses not to fight it, it seems to me that that relieves you from having to mutter and weep in your musty study in twenty or forty years about how close you came to winning.

I do not want to be remembered as a soldier. Simons Manigault, whatever else he was, was not a soldier in life. You may call him a momma's boy. He went AWOL, following his mother, not his father—absent with opprobrious love. He deigned not the Wawer, in all its aspects. He surrendered early.